W9-BFK-550

Tough Tiffany

Tough Tiffany

BELINDA HURMENCE

Doubleday & Company, Inc.
Garden City, New York

Library of Congress Cataloging in Publication Data
Hurmence, Belinda.
Tough Tiffany.
SUMMARY: Eleven-year-old Tiffany, youngest member of a poor family in rural North Carolina, takes her first steps toward adulthood.
[1. Family life—Fiction. 2. Poverty—Fiction] I. Title.
PZ7.H9567To [Fic]
ISBN: 0-385-15082-2 Trade
ISBN: 0-385-15083-0 Prebound
Library of Congress Catalog Card Number 79-6979

PRINTED IN THE UNITED STATES OF AMERICA

for Howard

Contents

Tough Tiffany

1

Born Cute

The house looked like other houses on Swenson Street, propped on crumbling brick piers, its face shaded by a tin roof that swept down over the porch. Inside, on a chilly April evening, a gangling young girl with rather large ears and beautifully plaited cornrows energetically jumped and wrote. Tiffany Cox is tall and tough, said Tiffany Cox to herself. With a piece of chalk, a stroke for each leap, she wrote on the plasterboard ceiling: TIF.

Mama yelled from the kitchen, "Tiff, what I tell you about jumping on those beds?"

Tiff pretended not to hear, but she hastily got down and crawled under the front bed and thumped around among the battered corrugated boxes shoved there.

Mama opened the bedroom door. "You hear me talken?"

Tiff backed out from beneath the bed, bumping one of the cartons along with her. "Ma'am?" she said innocently.

"Jumping up and down on the beds."

"I was just looking for my Thilly sweat shirt." Tiff plowed earnestly through the contents of the box. "Yay! I found it!"

"I hear you. How come the bedspread all mess up?"

"Mama, you know I have to stand in the bed when I go to spread it. How'm I going to get over to the back wall without I walk on the bedspread?"

Some days you could fool Mama, other days she'd switch you for breathing. Today she said merely, "I catch you breaking down them bed slats, you get a bed slat broke across you backside," and she stalked back to the kitchen singing, "Lord, Don't Move My Mountain" in her abrasive, thready voice.

Tiff breathed out. Just since Thanksgiving she had grown a lot—two and a half inches in four months—and maybe more to come. Looked like she had it made on tall. Tough would take a while longer, unless she figured some way of outguessing Mama.

Tiffany and her twin sisters, Lena and Lana, and her half sisters, Denise and Dawn, all slept together in two sway-backed metal beds that filled up their room. A lean-to cubicle off the kitchen at one time served the house as closet and storeroom, but Mama and Daddy took it for their bedroom so the girls could have the real bedroom, and Dude, the only boy in the family, slept in the front room on the couch. That was why they kept clothes and things under the metal beds in grocery store cartons—though not always in the proper cartons.

Rummaging in her box, Tiff discovered one of her

half sister Denise's sandals, and she flung this into another box under the bed. She found also her half sister Dawn's math book left over from when she had to repeat last year in summer school. Tiff thumbed through to see how hard the problems were. Plenty hard. Toward the back of the book the pages parted to reveal an envelope, taped so it wouldn't fall out of the book. Another piece of tape secured the flap, but Tiff delicately peeled it back without skinning the flap. Inside, she found a boy's picture inscribed, "Love ya—Joe." Tiff gagged. "Love" she could ignore, but "Love ya" was throw-up stuff. Joe himself looked like the kind of guy Granny Turner would say was a nice boy, wide flat nose on a wide serious face and his scalp shining silvery black through a skinny haircut.

The math book was Dawn's, but the photo belonged to Denise, elder of the half sisters. Dawn must have secretly removed it from the pack in Denise's box. Boys were always giving Denise their pictures. Occasionally she might tape one up on the plywood wall of their room, but usually she just shuffled them carelessly together with a rubber band around.

Tiff replaced the photograph and resealed the envelope. She searched through the cartons beneath the beds until she found one with mostly Dawn's clothes in it and thrust the math book into a wad of underwear.

Denise and Dawn complained about how their clothes got wrinkled in the boxes and how they had to iron what they were going to wear to school every morning.

Tiff and the twins didn't care whether their clothes were ironed or not. In fact, Tiff couldn't understand why Dawn and Denise did, for they put on the wrinkledest, patched-upest, worn-outest old jeans they owned, but the blouses they wore over them they ironed and ironed till they looked perfect, like they just come from the store. Mama said that was the way everybody did in high school, and Tiff and the twins would do that way too when they got to be in high school.

Tiff liked old jeans herself, but instead of a shirt or blouse she preferred her two pretty pink sweat shirts that they both of them said THOCK IT TO ME, BABY across the front. She had run across them in one of the boxes under the double beds, and the twins said sure, she could have them, they never liked them anyway. Never liked them! Tiff loved those sweat shirts so much she could tell them apart, the way she could tell the twins apart, even though they were exactly alike twins and exactly alike sweat shirts. She named one sweat shirt Thtupid. It was her lucky sweat shirt. She always wore Thtupid when she was going to have a test in school. The other, named Thilly, was neither lucky nor unlucky, but she loved Thilly best because it hugged her in a way Thtupid never did, quite.

Uncle Flake, Mama's brother, had brought the twins the sweat shirts for a joke, back when they were a lot littler and couldn't pronounce their s's. Uncle Flake thought it was so cute the way Lena and Lana couldn't say their s's, and he about died laughing when Lena said resentfully, "I think that'th thtupid," and Lana said, "I think it'th thilly," and neither of them would thank Uncle Flake for the present, even though it was a free present, not for their birthday or Easter Monday or anything else, just free. Uncle Flake was Mama's richest brother, if you didn't count Uncle George Harvey in New York. He lived in Toadtown and had a car that was nearly paid for that he sometimes took them to church in.

Lena and Lana refused to wear the sweat shirts. They stuffed them in a box and threw old dirty sneakers on top of them and pushed the box under the beds way far back against the wall; and Lena said, "Th-th-th-ths-s-s."

"H-h-hs-s-s-s," said Lana.

"Thstupid," Lena said.

"Hsilly!"

The twins hissed at each other, and hissed and hissed all that day and all weekend, and that was the way they finally learned to say their s's. Uncle Flake would tell the story just about every time he saw Tiff wearing one of the pink sweat shirts, and he still thought it was funny and he would die laughing and tell Lena and Lana they ought to thank him for learning them to say their s's; but they never thanked him for it, though maybe they ought to have.

Tiff and Lena and Lana slept together in the bed against the back wall, because they were the littlest and didn't need as much room as Dawn and Denise. For a long time Tiff and the twins could sleep sideways on their bed and have plenty of room, but when the twins got taller they had to turn around longways and after that they argued a lot about who had to sleep in the middle. Tiff always lost, and it wasn't because she was younger or smaller (although she *was* younger and used to be shorter), but because you never could win against twins—it was two against one. That was unfair, two against one. Yet Tiff didn't object often, because other people were unfair to Lena and Lana; and it evened out. "Aren't they cute?" people said (for twins were just naturally born cute), and they never said about one twin, "Isn't she cute?" What they said about one twin was, "I can't tell which one of you is which. Are you Lena or Lana?"

Well, nobody ever said, "Isn't Tiff cute?" either, and no wonder, for she wasn't born cute and it looked like she wouldn't ever grow up cute, but at least people didn't ask her what her name was all the time. If they recognized her at all, they knew she was Tiffany.

2

Born Curious

Whenever something was lost in the Coxes' house, it usually ended up being found in one of the boxes under the beds. "Who's got my notebook?" Lana would yell, or Tiff would ask her half brother, Dude, "Did you take my bubble gum?" and Mama would say right off, "Go look under the bed before you cuse anybody."

Trouble was, nobody wanted to look under the bed; there was too much junk there. Everybody was supposed to keep their stuff in their own box, but everybody except Tiff had more than one, and when they got in a hurry looking for what they wanted, they would pull things out of first one box and then another and pile them all back in together any old way.

Times when Mama screamed about straightening up the house, they'd throw everything under the bed that happened to be laying around, no matter who it belonged to. Tiff found Daddy's tire iron in her box one time, and little bitty things like nail clippers and combs slid down in corners to the bottom, so when you were looking for a sock that would match or a clean undershirt, you could nearly always find something fun to try out, like blue nail polish or Denise's false eyelashes.

That evening, just before supper, Dawn whined, "Mama, Tiffany been messing my hair cream again."

Mama said, "Tiff, how many times I tell you stop messing?"

"I wasn't messing, Mama, it was in my box. Can't I use something that's in my own box?"

Dawn said, "How you think my stuff get in your box, the tooth fairy put it in there?"

Tiff felt like asking Dawn if the tooth fairy put Joe's picture in her math book, but she didn't want to admit to snooping. Anyway, she felt sorry for Dawn making out on Denise's boy friend, that Denise didn't even like. She never asked him for his picture in the first place.

Mama said, "I don't care if it was in your box, you not sposed to mess with your sisters' stuff. Your daddy going to bust your butt when he come home. You just naturally a born messing child."

"Born curious," said Tiff with a smirk.

"Say what?"

"Born curious. That's what Ms. Lackey says about me at school. Nearly every day she says it, 'Tiffany, you were born curious,' she says."

Mama frowned. "I don't like to hear that, Tiffany. Messing at home is one thing, but you get a beating for messing at school, that's serious."

"Oh, Ms. Lackey isn't going to beat me, Mama, not

me or anybody else. Ms. Lackey likes it for me to be curious, I can tell."

Her half brother, Dude, sneered, "You can tell she likes you cause she didn't beat you yet." Dude, in junior high, sneered a lot.

"I can tell," said Tiff haughtily, "by the way she says it, like she's proud of me figuring out things. 'Tiffany, you always figuring out,' she says."

"Well, you better go *watching* out, is the way *I* says it," said Mama.

When Daddy came home, Tiff heard her saying to him, "I'm going to buy us some bunk beds for the girls' room, they got just the ones I want down at the Outlet Furniture place, with a real nice bureau that matches and a mirror onto it. They need they own place for keeping things, growing up so fast, and particularly they need they own bed."

"Yes, particularly Dawn. She growing up particularly fast," said Daddy. He struck his lean finger in one ear and waggled it, the way he did when he thought he was being funny.

"Honey, I don't like you joking about Dawn. You know that. Also, I don't want the other chaps hearing you."

"How come? You think they blind or something?"

"You hush that up. Help me figure out a way we can buy us those bunk beds, for I mean to do it. Yes, sir, I am definitely going to buy those bunk beds."

Mama's eyes sparkled and she began talking rapidly in

the higher voice she used when she was fixing to buy something. Daddy shook his head in disgust, the way he always did when Mama talked like that. It didn't necessarily mean he was disgusted. Mostly he was proud of her for being so quick and smart. He was tall and slow and easy himself, and brisk little people like Mama amazed him. He had that astonished look a giraffe does, peering at littler creatures scurrying around, and a giraffe's cautious way of moving, like he hadn't quite got the hang of walking yet.

It would be exciting to get bunk beds in their room, Tiff thought. In her mind she rearranged the room and started figuring out a way to get a top bunk for herself; but common sense told her it was not going to happen. That was just Mama's talk. She was always going on about buying rich things, like a car or a stereo, but they never bought them. Or if they did buy something, the company would come and take it away again, like the telephones.

Last September, before Tiff went into fifth grade, Mama had two telephones installed—a green one in the kitchen and a blue one by her bed—just across the corner from each other, unfortunately, so it was impossible to listen in on a conversation without the other party knowing about it. Even so it was great, not having to go up to the Laundromat when you needed to make a phone call. Pretty soon, though, the telephone company came and took the telephones out. Tiff wished there could have been some way to keep them, like Mama did sometimes when the company came to cut off their electric, borrowing from the rent money out of the hiding place, or borrowing from Uncle Flake or Granny or Aunt Sister.

But Mama said she decided telephones weren't worth the trouble they caused, everybody calling you up all the time, you couldn't get a lick of work done around the house. She said if they got a telephone again she would ask for an unlisted number. Tiff hoped not. It was good to see your name in print. Months after the telephones had been disconnected, she still looked up their number in the old Silasville directory:

Cox Robt D 395 Swnsn Av——————**NQ3-5611**

Why didn't they write Daddy's whole name out? she wondered. And their address? Plenty of room. Instead, they put four abbreviations on that one line alone, with no periods to show they were abbreviations, not even a comma between Cox and Robt. If Tiff wrote like that in class, you could just figure how her paper would look when she got it back from Ms. Lackey grading it. Red marks all over the place!

What Mama said to Daddy got her curious, and she asked the twins, "Do you think Dawn is growing up any faster than we are?"

"Not faster, fatter," Lana replied. Lana was supposed to be the humorous twin. Tiff told them the conversation she had overheard about the bunk beds, and Lana said, "Dawn so fat Mama have to buy her *two* bunk beds, one for her butt and one for her gut." It sounded so funny the way she said it, they hollered laughing; but they didn't laugh long, because they felt mean in their hearts, laughing about their own half sister, though it was true about her being fat. They were all of them thin, except for Dawn, Tiff especially. Since Thanksgiving she had gotten so long-legged and funny-looking that Lana compared her pert little rump jutting out high above the ground to marshmallows on toasting sticks. "*Burnt* marshmallows," said Lana, the humorous twin. Whenever she could, Tiff wore bulky sweat shirts and hid her birdy legs with blue jeans. There wasn't much she could do about her big ears and her big mouth. Mama said when she filled out a little they wouldn't look so prominent.

Lena said, "Mama's not going to buy us any bunk beds. She just talking, you know Mama."

"Yeah," said Lana.

"We know." Tiff sighed.

But were they ever wrong about Mama! When they came home from school the next day, they found the Outlet Furniture van backed up to their front door, and their double beds already taken apart and stacked outside on the front porch. Inside, the boxes that held their belongings huddled together in the middle of the suddenly gigantic room. Tiff's underpants lay embarrassingly exposed, and she hastily piled her schoolbooks on top to hide them from view, just as the moving men carried in the first bunk.

"Where you want this, ma'am?" asked one of the men.

"Along that wall, I guess," said Mama. "No, let me think—how about with the head against the wall and the foot sticking out?"

"Whatever you say, ma'am," said the man politely, and he shoved aside a box to set the first bunk in place.

Mama said, "That doesn't look right; you better turn it around longways of the wall." The men turned it as she directed and tramped out for another bunk.

Tiff said, "I figured out a good way to put the bunks, Mama."

"Don't bother me whiles I'm trying to think!" said Mama distractedly.

Tiff began pulling boxes into the front room to make way for the moving men. Mama had bought two sets of bunk beds made of pretty brown speckled wood, with a ladder for each top bunk; and each set had a matching bureau with attached mirror. The mattresses were all flowerdy pink and blue and yellow, so pretty you wouldn't want to cover them up with sheets. Mama couldn't make up her mind how to place the bunks in their room, and the moving men finally just lined them three in a row where their old beds had stood, and jammed the fourth with the bureaus in the front room. Mama said she would be able to think better after the moving men were gone.

Denise and Dude came in from school and began to

say how they thought the bunks should be arranged, and they stacked up a pair to see how they would look.

"The way I figure, it's like sleeping on a shelf," said Tiff.

"Where can we put the bureaus?" Lena asked.

Mama was disappointed. "I sure thought there would be more room in here than there is. I can't see a place for but one of those bureaus on that back wall. What'll we do with the extra one? No room for it in the front room."

"Let me tell you my idea," said Tiff.

"Nothing is going to work," said Denise. "Mama thought by stacking up the bunks we'd save space, but we don't, because we need so much more room for the bureaus."

Tiff said, "But *one* bunk bed is a lot smaller than two double beds. And there's plenty of room going up to the ceiling."

"What do you mean by that?"

"I mean, instead of two sets of bunks, we can stack them all up like one set of shelves. See, they're made to fit on top of each other. Daddy can fasten the ladders together so we can reach the top bunk."

"You know," said Dude, "you aren't as dumb as you look!"

Dawn came in just as they got the last bunk boosted up, and watched in silence while they carried in the new bureaus and arranged them against the opposite wall. What a difference it was going to make! No more crawling under the beds, searching for the right box. No more standing in the beds to spread them. No more climbing over a row of sleeping sisters when you had to get up in the night. They could actually walk around in their room now, and they had eight huge drawers in the new bureaus to put their clothes in. Tiff figured it out: two each for Denise and Dawn, because they were the oldest, one and one-half each for Lana and Lena, and one for herself.

"I'm taking the top drawers," Dawn announced gruffly.

Denise said, "Seems to me like Tiff ought to get first pick, since she only asked for one drawer herself."

"Oh, sure, give the baby first pick, that's the way you always do, just because she's the littlest!"

Tiff said, "I don't care which one I get. You can have the top drawers if you want, Dawnie."

"I call for the top bunk!" Lena and Lana spoke simultaneously.

Denise said, "Let's draw straws for the top bunk. That's the fairest way."

But Mama said fair didn't have anything to do with it, and she assigned the bunks according to her own system, Tiff on top because she was the lightest, Dawn on the bottom because she was heaviest, Lena and Lana sharing the second bunk, and Denise in the third. Tiff tried not to show how pleased she was with the assignment. Nobody else liked it, but Mama said she didn't want any of their mouth, and she went out to the kitchen to set supper.

"Well, anyway, our room looks nice," said Denise. She began transferring her things into the new bureau.

Lena said, "You know what, Lana? We can sleep my head at one end of the bed and yours at the other, and our feet will only overlap a little bit in the middle."

Dawn brought clean sheets and threw them onto the bottom bunk. She kept her face turned away, making up the new bed, but Tiff could tell from her back that she was crying. There was something about the rigid way she held her shoulders. In a family you always knew those things. She said softly, "I'll trade bunks with you, Dawnie."

"I don't want your old bunk!"

The twins whirled. "Is she crying?"

"No!"

"Yes you are, too. Turn around and look at us if you're not crying. You are too crying. What are you crying about, Dawn?"

"Leave me alone! Why don't you leave me alone?" And Dawn wrenched away and ran out to lock herself in the bathroom.

"What's the matter of her?" asked Dude.

3

What's the Matter with Dawn?

Right after supper, Dude put on his pajamas and curled up on the couch in the front room to watch TV. The twins joined him, for it was Dawn and Denise's turn to do the dishes, but Tiff brought her homework out to the kitchen table where the light was good. They were studying China in her class now, and she was drawing symbols on the outline of a map to show where the biggest cities and the mountains and rivers were, and what people ate and did for a living. The mountains and rivers were easiest, a few humps for the mountains and squiggles for the rivers; but the other symbols were more fun to draw. Out in the ocean she put little boats with square sails, and on the shore she showed a man with slanty eyes and a pigtail catching a fish. Inland, she drew rice piled in a blue bowl, which she had copied from a grits box.

Denise looked over her shoulder. "What's that sticking out of the grits?"

"Chopsticks," replied Tiff, "and that's rice, not grits. In China they use chopsticks to eat their rice and hencefish."

"Rice and how much?"

"Hencefish."

"Never heard of any fish called like that."

"It's the kind of fish they eat there." She read aloud from her social studies book, 'Hence fish and rice are the principal foods in the rich Yangtze basin.'"

Denise examined the passage. "You dummy, that's two words! They're talking about where it comes from, fish from the river and rice from the plain. '*Hence*,' you see, '*fish and rice are the—*'"

"Okay, okay, I get it now," Tiff said rapidly. The mistake was humiliating, for she was considered the best reader of the family. No hope of concealing it now; Dude and the twins crowded into the kitchen to see what Denise was laughing about. Denise explained the error in loving detail.

"All *right*, I said," Tiff repeated. "All I did was read it too fast. What's so funny about that?"

"Thusfish." Dude giggled. "Hence means *thus*, doesn't it?"

"Or *so*," said Lana, also giggling. "Sofish and rice, that's what they eat."

"It means *therefore*, too," Denise supplied, and Lana, clowning, said, "Now, *therefore*, class, what kind of fish do they eat in China?"

"Thereforefish!" they chorused.

"I know, I know, I know! I'm so funny I ought to be on television!" Tiff laughed loudly. She was grateful she had made the mistake at home instead of in school. In school, if you made that kind of mistake, sometimes kids would try to get you mad or hurt your feelings so there would be that much more to laugh about. Once a teacher (not Ms. Lackey, of course) laughed with the kids until Tiff actually cried a little bit, and the teacher said, "Why, Tiffany, that isn't anything to cry about, where's your sense of humor?" When she got onto having a sense of humor, she saw right away there were plenty of other kids like her who learned to laugh it up when really they felt like crying.

After the dishes had been washed and wiped and put away, they all went into the front room and watched TV for a while. Daddy had his box of scrap metal and bolts strewn over the floor, where he worked at fastening the two bunk-bed ladders together. Mama, with the dustpan, divided her attention between a TV comedian and sweeping up after Daddy. Dude curled up again with his blanket and pillow on the couch, which was his bed at night. He often fell asleep watching TV, and that was why he liked to put on his pajamas right after supper; when they finally turned the set off, they needn't wake him.

The comedian on TV was telling a joke about a fat lady weighing herself on a machine that was wired for sound, and Dude said sleepily, "Dawn better not get on one of those machines."

Lana mimicked the comedian: "'One at a time, please, lady!'"

Tiff stole a glance at Dawn, hunched at the foot of the couch, picking a fingernail in the flickering light of television. Her plump cheeks squeezed her eyes nearly shut.

"Dawn, you getting so fat," Dude exclaimed. "You better look out how you sit on my bed, you don't break it down."

"Leave her alone," said Denise.

The twins turned willingly from the television, looking for diversion. Dawn stonily examined her hands.

"She crying again," Dude announced. "What she all time crying for?"

Denise said furiously, "You ever think of minding your own business?"

Dude pulled himself into a tight ball. Denise was beautiful and smart and admired by everybody, not least by himself. "Well, I just asking what's the matter of her," he said defensively.

"Nothing the *matter* of her," Mama said, with a sudden scornful glance at Dawn.

Daddy said unexpectedly, "That's enough, now! Any more this talk, somebody gets their butt broke, I don't care who it is. You hear me?"

Tiff tried not to stare at Dawn, but she couldn't help herself. Her thick shoulders humped once, and she struggled to heave her cumbersome body from the sway-backed couch. She made not a sound, though tears poured shining from her eyes.

"Robert, I told you before," Mama was saying, "not in front of the chaps—" as Dawn disappeared into the bedroom and closed the door behind her.

"What you mean, not in front of the chaps? If they don't know already, then it's time somebody told them, and if you don't tell them, I'm going to."

Denise said in a bored voice, "We already know, Daddy Robert."

"Know what?" said Lena. "I don't know anything."

"Me neither," Lana chimed in. "What you talking about?"

"What's happen?" Dude asked.

Tiff slipped into the bedroom after Dawn without waiting to hear more. Whatever it was, she didn't want to stay in the front room talking and maybe laughing about Dawn behind her back.

Her sister faced her with bitter eyes. "I hope you satisfied," she said. "Maybe if you all gang up on me, you can send me to jail."

Tiff stopped short. Jail? Had Dawn stolen something? She did borrow things without asking, Denise's hair rollers and her earrings. That picture of Joe concealed in her math book, that was something more than borrowing, wasn't it? Even though Denise wouldn't have cared and probably didn't notice the photograph had vanished. "I'm not ganging up on you, Dawn," she declared. "I came in here to see if you wanted me to help you."

Dawn turned away. "Can't anybody help me," she said hopelessly. "Mama so mad at me, I'd run away if I knew where to go, but that still wouldn't help me, oh, oh, oh." She lowered herself onto the bottom bunk bed and buried her face in the pillow.

Tiff felt like crying too. It was just awful the way Dawn kept crying all the time. She had to figure out some way to make her stop doing that, because if she kept on, she was going to make herself sick. "Don't cry, Dawnie, please don't cry," she pleaded, and she laid her cheek against her sister's shoulder and petted her. "Can't be anything so bad your own family can't help you. Daddy's not mad at you, couldn't you tell that? He's mad at the rest of us for cutting up."

"No he's not. He doesn't care. Why should he care? He's not my real daddy."

Tiff was shocked. Of course she knew, they all did, that Dawn's daddy, and Denise's and Dude's, was somebody from long time ago, before Mama married Daddy. But long time ago didn't count, compared to right now. Daddy was right now. He was real. "That's not fair," she protested. "Daddy loves you the same as me and the twins, and Denise and Dude too. He treats us all alike."

"It's not Denise and Dude he's mad at; it's me. You're his own flesh and blood, so you don't know what it's like, but I do, because we're not."

"You can't say Mama isn't your own flesh and blood mama," Tiff argued reasonably.

"She's mad too. She's madder at me than Daddy Robert is."

"Well, why don't you try to make up with them? Doesn't seem to me like you're even trying. Can't you say you're sorry and you'll pay it back or something?"

"Sorry! How you think you pay back a baby?"

Tiff was confused. "I don't know what you mean. Which baby?"

"The one I'm going to have, dummy. Can't you tell I'm going to have a baby? Don't you have any sense at all?"

"Oh no!" Tiff was shocked. "Oh, Dawn! That's terrible."

Dawn slumped pathetically, and Tiff wanted to bite her tongue out.

"Knock knock," said Daddy, at the door. "Let's see if that terrific idea of yours is going to work." He brought in the spliced ladder and hooked it in place along the top bunk railing. "There. Try that out. If you break your neck, we'll need another terrific idea." He waggled his finger in his ear.

Tiff scurried up and down the ladder several times, grateful for the interruption, while Daddy watched critically.

"Ladder's stronger than that stack of beds," he pronounced. "Let me see if I can't anchor those posts into the wall studs." He fetched his tools and the box of bolts and screws and began drilling and hammering. Dawn pulled a nightgown from her bureau drawer and left the room.

From the top bunk, Tiff watched Daddy work. Slow and easy was Daddy, but he never had to backtrack, and once he got a thing fixed, you knew it was fixed for good.

"Well, there. Maybe it's not the prettiest job in the world," he conceded when the bunks had been secured to the wall, "but if they fall down in the night, you can wake me up and tell me about it." Tiff handed down his brace and bit and rolled over on her back as he went out.

It was like a room of her own, up there under the ceiling. There wasn't enough clearance for her to sit up, but she didn't mind that. The single bulb that dangled from a center cord shed a harsh light in the room, but the same light, reflecting against the ceiling, bathed her snug new kingdom with a soft and luminous glow. She snuggled up against the wall. Anybody coming into the room would have to climb the ladder to know for sure she was up there. And it was her bed, her private bed! She had never slept in a private bed in her life. The light was just right for reading in bed, something she knew about only from books and never dreamed she would be able to do. Blissfully she sighed.

From the ceiling, her name unexpectedly winked at her, TIF, the letters she had chalked on the plasterboard yesterday, jumping up and down on the old beds. How long ago that seemed! She reached out languidly and erased the chalk marks with her finger tips. By stretching a bit, she could touch the light cord. Imagine being able to cut off the light without getting out of bed! She practiced locating the cord in the dark and turning the switch on, off, on. Off. In the dark, she relished her new privacy all the more. Television laughter drifted to her ears like a message from another planet, star people trying to communicate with her. Then the door opened and Dawn's heavy tread communicated reality instead.

She lay rigid waiting for Dawn to say something, but she didn't. She simply got into bed in the dark and lay there. Maybe she was listening for star people too. No. Dawn said herself there wasn't anybody could help her now.

"I'll help you, Dawnie," Tiff called out impulsively. "Don't you worry, I'll figure out a way."

After a startled silence Dawn spoke. "I didn't know you were up there." Presently she added, despairingly, "You think you so tough. You don't know nothing."

Tiff quailed. Dawn was right, she didn't know anything. But somebody had to do something to help Dawn. "You just wait and see," she said boldly. "I'm going to figure out a way tomorrow. You'll see."

4

Teachers Don't Know Everything

One lousy mistake! Dawn's whole life was changed! Tiff wore Thtupid, her lucky sweat shirt, to school the next morning, for she had resolved to talk to Ms. Lackey about Dawn, and that was like a test she didn't know the answers to, so she needed all the luck she could get. There never had been a test in school that she dreaded as much as she dreaded this one.

Tiff knew everything about babies, how they got inside the mothers and grew until they were ready to come out. What she hadn't figured much about were the fathers, but instead had vaguely assumed that fathers were always husbands as well, and that made mothers wives.

But Dawn wasn't a wife. Imagine Dawn being a wife! She was just barely fifteen and still played Monopoly and jacks with Tiff and the twins. No, that was wrong.

Dawn hadn't played any games with them for a long long time. Now that Tiff thought it over, her sweet sister, who taught her to plait crazy cornrows, who used to whisper secrets, hardly talked any more. Instead she cried, silently, and somehow they had all grown used to her silence and her tears. Tiff, the curious one, had never thought to ask why she was crying.

Oh, but why did she ask? She didn't want to know about Dawn. She hated knowing! For a moment, Tiff puzzled with an interesting realization: you could always find out something you wanted to know bad enough; yet once you knew, no matter how you wished you could go back, there was no way of *not* knowing.

"Who is the father of the baby?" Ms. Lackey asked, and Tiff told her about Joe.

Tiff just loved Ms. Lackey. She was the best teacher Tiff ever had, best teacher in the whole world probably, and the best-looking. If she cut off her hair, you could just count on some other teachers cutting off theirs right away. One day she wore two scarves around her neck, and before the week was over, practically everybody was wearing two scarves around their neck. Just the way her face hollowed when she said the word "oh" always made Tiff suck in her cheeks.

And smart! This morning, when she decided she couldn't do it after all, couldn't talk to her about Dawn, Ms. Lackey found a time for saying confidentially, "Is there something you'd like to talk to me about, Tiffany?" and she was so nice, and so plain, that Tiff could tell her everything without feeling like a tattletale, or ashamed, or worried. Ms. Lackey said it might help her not to worry if she could talk to an older woman, like her mother maybe; and she didn't make Tiff feel rotten about saying it was no use talking to Mama, because Mama always got nervous and excited and yelled.

"Most mothers do feel nervous at times," Ms. Lackey said. "They think it's their fault if their children are unhappy."

Privately, Tiff thought it *was* Mama's fault Dawn was unhappy; the baby was bad, of course, but Mama yelling about it made things worse. Ms. Lackey seemed to grab these thoughts right out of Tiff's head. "It helps if girls can remember their mothers do love them, and strictness is a way of showing they care," she said.

That Mama acted hateful to Dawn because she loved her was an odd idea, and Tiff stuck it in a corner of her mind for thinking over later on. She had planned on talking about Dawn, not Mama. Yet here they were, and she couldn't think of one thing to say, or ask. A long silence bothered her. On a test, if she didn't know the answer, she would always put something in the blank space, even if she knew it was wrong. So now, inadequately, she said, "I'm only Dawn's half sister. Will that make me a half aunt?"

Ms. Lackey looked thoughtful. Probably she didn't know. Teachers didn't know everything. When she finally did speak, it was not to answer but to ask about something else. "How do you feel about the baby, Tiffany?" she said.

"I hate it," Tiff said promptly. "It's going to be all ugly and sneaky, like Joe. I hope Dawn makes him take it, when it gets born, and keep it over at his house. There isn't any room for a baby in our house. Even with our bunk beds, Lena and Lana have to sleep together. Besides, Dawn doesn't want any baby that makes everybody mad at her and she cries all the time about it."

"How does Dawn feel about Joe?"

"She doesn't like him any more. He never was her boy friend, anyway. It was Denise he was always hanging around and trying to get her to be his steady girl friend. But everybody wants Neesie to be their steady girl friend because she's so pretty and smart."

"Isn't Dawn pretty and smart?"

Tiff considered. "Maybe. But she doesn't think she is. She makes jokes about how she is fat and dumb—she used to make jokes, I mean. Now all she does is cry. *I* don't care if she's fat. She feels nice and soft when she hugs me. I want her to go back being the way she was. She does too, I bet."

Tiff stopped talking. That was it. That was what she wanted Ms. Lackey to tell her—how to get Dawn back the way she was before she started having this baby.

Ms. Lackey said Dawn ought to be going to the doctor for checkups. She talked about how important her diet was, vitamins and minerals, things like that, nothing

Tiff wanted to hear; and she spoke of caring for the baby after it was born. But all Tiff cared about the baby being after it was born was out of sight. Joe ought to take it so Dawn could be happy again.

But Ms. Lackey said little babies needed somebody with them all time and a young boy like Joe would not understand an infant's needs.

Tiff said, "Huh! That's his tough greens. He should have thought of that before he talked Dawn into making the baby."

Things didn't work that way, Ms. Lackey argued. It was a mistake to make the baby, she agreed, but it was done. So Dawn had to plan for the future now. Did she mean to finish high school? Would she place the baby for adoption? If she kept the baby after it was born, she would have to think of where the money to support them both would come from. There were so many things to be considered, she said, that it was hard for her to advise Tiff without talking to Dawn herself.

Ms. Lackey was one smart teacher, but she sure didn't know everything. While she talked of vitamins and high school and doctors, things that weren't really going to help Dawn any, Tiff's mind took little pieces of what she was thinking and little pieces of what Ms. Lackey was saying, and figured out the perfect answer. It happened that way sometimes.

"If I can help," Ms. Lackey said when the bell rang, "if she would like me to talk to her guidance counselor or go with her to the Welfare office–"

"Yes, ma'am, I'll tell her," said Tiff, already planning out her idea. It was the obvious answer, so obvious she felt dumb it hadn't occurred to her immediately. Settling in her desk after the bell rang, she rubbed her chest joyfully. "Thtupid old sweat shirt," she said.

5

Over to Aunt Sister's

As soon as school was out, Tiff walked over to the high school and waited on the front steps for Dawn. Denise came out first, with three boys and another girl. Neesie always had a crowd to walk home with. She was friendly to everybody. Tiff tried to be like her, but it was hard going. Maybe there were more losers in fifth grade than there were in high school.

"Hey, Tiff," said Denise, looking pleased, "you waiting for me?"

"Well"–Tiff was reluctant to say no–"for you and Dawn."

"Okay. Want to go to the Lotta Burger with us?"

She meant it. Denise never minded her kid sister trailing along with her crowd. It was tempting; oh my, think of a strawberry slurpy on a day like this! But Tiff had something else on her mind, and the Lotta Burger was out of the way, so she said regretfully, "I thought we might go over to Aunt Sister's."

"Oh," said Denise. She looked closely at Tiff. "*Oh,*"

as if they shared some understanding. "Want me to go too?" Then, not waiting for an answer, she added, "You don't need me. We can go for a slurpy tomorrow. Tell Aunt Sister, hey, hear?" Two girls and another boy ran down the steps to join her crowd, and they all walked off, a chattering, cheerful mob. It looked like so much fun. Tiff felt let down, watching them go. This must be the way Dawn felt all the time.

Dawn trudged out alone. She looked tired and messy. Although she was fat, Dawn was usually prissy about her appearance. There wasn't anybody could plait cornrows to suit her. She was the only girl Tiff knew who could plait in back of her own head.

"Where are your books?" asked Tiff.

"In there." Dawn jerked her head backward at the school building. "I don't need them any more. I'm not going back."

"Oh, Dawnie."

"Well, I'm not. Don't you start. The guidance counselor called me in today and asked me if I was pregnant."

Tiff thought of what Ms. Lackey said about talking to an older woman. "Maybe the counselor could help you." she said. "What did you tell her?"

"I told her no, I wasn't," said Dawn. She seemed about to cry, but with enormous effort she managed to pretend interest in Tiff. "What are you doing here?"

"I came to see if you'd like to walk over to Aunt Sister's with me."

Dawn hated walking. Sometimes she joked about it, saying she had Cadillac tastes, but in fact walking was uncomfortable for her. It chafed her thighs and made her calves ache. Aunt Sister lived in Toadtown, the poorest section of the city, and that meant more than a mile of walking, all of it hilly, plus walking home afterward. Dawn picked at a fingernail. "Well"—she gave Tiff the same glance Denise had, as if they shared some understanding—"okay."

They set off together, past the classroom annex in back, skirting the sports field and cutting through the parking lot to Catawba Street. That led out to where Free Mary Creek divided Toadtown from the rest of Silasville. Toadtown was not a real town, but only a section in Silasville, the way Swenson Street, where Tiff's family lived, was. To say you lived in Swenson Street did not necessarily mean your house was located on that street; rather it described who you were, and what your status was, according to the areas of the city. Swenson Street, for example, was not as poor a section as Toadtown, but the people who lived there were poorer than those in Honeycutt, some of whom owned their own houses. Tiff's Granny Turner lived in Honeycutt.

"How come they call Toadtown Toadtown?" Tiff wondered.

"It's where Free Mary lived," said Dawn.

"I know Free Mary lived there, but Free Mary wasn't any toad, was she?"

For reply, Dawn merely grunted.

Free Mary, they both knew, was a freed slave who had lived in her own cabin on her own ground out in the country near the creek named after her. Silasville had grown out to the country even before Free Mary died, and modern city streets surrounded the once-proud little freehold. Who remembered now where Mary's cabin had stood? Her land was crowded with rows of crumbling rent houses—the first stopping place for county folks who wanted to move in. Most of the streets in Toadtown were still dirt streets, though the city streets of Silasville surrounding it had long since been paved.

"Coming up a storm," said Dawn. "We better scoot."

They scurried onto Aunt Sister's ramshackle front porch as the first drops fell. "Get in this house, you chaps!" Aunt Sister bellowed. "Storm got to blow you here fore you come visiting?"

Aunt Sister wasn't much older than Mama, who was the baby of the Turner family, but she acted almost as old as Granny Turner, and every bit as bossy. Still, nobody minded Aunt Sister's bossing. Granny Turner had got fed up with little babies by the time Uncle Flake and Mama came along, so Aunt Sister mothered them. Out of habit, she still fussed over Mama and Uncle Flake, her precious babies. Short in stature, she billowed from the top down—cheeks, chin, bosom, belly—in folds of flesh that seemed designed to cushion all babies from the shocks of the world. She was Aunt Sister to every child except her own. Tiff wasn't sure she had any other name.

A small flock of cousins and other children swirled around the guests. Aunt Sister hustled them into the tiny front room, hugging them both at the same time and bestowing great smacking kisses. Then she stood back and surveyed Dawn's body, arms akimbo. "Child, child," she mourned, "why you never come tell Aunt Sister this trouble?"

But she did not pause for answer. They all knew what to do in the face of impending storm. "Dawn, you cut off the TV," Aunt Sister directed. "Bruv, go unplug the fridge. Rest of you chaps round us up some chairs, and Tiff, you help me pull the babies back from the windows."

Around the dingy walls were ranged cribs of the five babies she cared for during the day. These Tiff and her aunt pulled to the center of the worn linoleum. Wooden chairs the cousins brought were placed protectively around the babies, and they all sat down in the murky light, backs to the windows, to wait out the storm.

It was always dark in Aunt Sister's house, as it always was in Tiff's. Shade were kept drawn and lights turned on only at night; there was something comfortable and saving about perpetual gloom, the unique privacy of a crowded dwelling. The peculiar twilight of storm charged the familiar dusk, however; instead of private, you felt separate.

Storms thrilled Tiff. I'm going to get you, the wind seemed to say. Listen! and it would wrench and wrestle the trees and the first fire of rain would burst the dirt and spatter it up, and beat it down again, and smear and melt it and carry it away—BAM! You'd think the house cracked open, else how did the lightning streak inside? (That one was close!) You wouldn't want a storm to hurt you or your family or your house, but how come, then, you wished you could look at it? Wanted to see it at the very worst, when that happened?

In her lifetime, Tiff had watched only three storms, and those by chance merely because Mama wasn't home. Once Dude told on her, how she stood right out on the porch looking at forked lightning, and Mama slapped her good for tempting the tempest. You were supposed to get as far away as you could from metal or anything electric; and if you talked, or looked in a mirror, it was said to draw the lightning. Even the babies seemed to understand the rules and lay large-eyed and still as eerie green-gray dusk enclosed them and rain slashed at the windows.

Aunt Sister just loved little babies. Mama said first thing she remembered as a child was Aunt Sister riding her on her hip under the persimmon tree and pretending to be her mama; and she wasn't but three years older! Now she had nine children of her own, the oldest two married and living in the county. When the youngest had grown out of diapers, she started taking in babies by the day for mothers who wanted to go out to work. She kept older children too; the house was always crowded with children of all ages; but the law didn't allow more than five at a time, so Aunt Sister made out that the extras had only dropped in to visit.

One time, a mother paid Aunt Sister to keep her baby while she went to work, but at the end of the week she ran off to California without telling where she was going. Aunt Sister took that little baby and kept it for her ownself, and loved it and bought it new clothes and playpretties. Then some way the Welfare found out about it, and they came to take the baby away. Aunt Sister said they couldn't have it, and she got hold of a big stick and just dared that Welfare woman to come in the house; so the Welfare woman went off and made a policeman come back with her and get the baby away from Aunt Sister.

Aunt Sister cried and cried and said she wanted to adopt the baby and begged them to let her keep it. The Welfare woman said no, because Aunt Sister wasn't any kin, and she should understand how she was just doing her job, which was to put the baby in an approved home (which Aunt Sister's wasn't) until they could locate the mother. Aunt Sister called the woman awful names, but it didn't do her one bit of good. It never did, with the Welfare; and no matter how Aunt Sister asked around to find out where the baby was, so she could go visit it and see if it remembered her and was all right, she never saw that baby again.

Thinking of the aunt's old grief, Tiff schemed to give her Dawn's baby, when it got born. The best way, of course, was to make Joe take it, but if he refused, then

Aunt Sister was the next best solution, for she was blood kin to Dawn, and the Welfare wouldn't have any excuse for breaking her heart, when she got attached to this new baby.

The storm ended as abruptly as it had begun, and Aunt Sister started shoving the cribs back in place and making plans for Dawn that exactly fitted in with Tiff's.

"What you know about babies, you nothing but a baby yourself!" she boomed. "What you want to do is stay over here with me and help out with these young'uns, that'll learn you better than books will ever do."

Dawn began, "I don't know if Mama—"

"Oh, your mama, I'll handle your mama. I been taken care your mama all her life. Didn't she never make no mistakes, I ast you? She give you a hard time, we gonna ast her about your own daddy that you never seen or know where he is." Before Dawn's hurt face, Aunt Sister softened, "Scuse me, honey, what I mean to say is, ain't no human alive but what has made mistakes, and your mama knows it good as any and wants to keep you from hurt, is all. She been through some hard times, you can't blame her wanting to spare you."

She asked Tiff to hand her a clean diaper and plucked one of the babies from its crib. How did she know which one needed changing without checking? She just did. A pan of soapy water stood always ready on top of the space heater. Aunt Sister sat down in the rocker and lifted the baby by its feet, washing its bottom and its face with the same rag and speaking impartially to her visitors, children, God, babies, and the world at large:

"Now it's not going to help you none to blame Joe, for it's a man's way to do what he feels like doing. Be a whole nother story if men took on the birthing!—cut on the TV, honey, it's like a funeral in here—(Lord, Master, spare us, I didn't go to name it!). Boy can't be all bad; you say he reckonizes his sponsibilities and payen the bills. (Tiff, you get any skinnier, you ears be wider'n you face.) Look at it smile, says 'Aunt Sister, I'm just a teensie tinesy baby.' Yes it is. Yes it *is*. Look at it smile!

"They not going to learn you babies out of books. Dawn, honey, you come stay with your Aunt Sister and learn babies like it is, like it really is. Soon as that baby gets here, you can go right on back and get your education, or a job, whichever you want. Law don't say I can't raise my own blood kin. Everything gonna be all right, yes, Lord, gonna be a-a-all *right!*"

All right, Tiff thought, with secret joy, and she rubbed her lucky sweat shirt—Thtupid did it again.

6

The Cotton-patch Twins

The house on Swenson Street became a different place, with Dawn spending most of her time at Aunt Sister's. She left the house early all through April and the hot days of May and made the long walk to Toadtown while it was still cool. Suppertime was over and the dishes done by the time she returned. Mama always saved back a platter for her, but most of the time she said she wasn't hungry, and Tiff and Dude would sometimes share out her portion of collards and corn bread before they went to bed. Some nights she slept over at Aunt Sister's, and those nights Lena and Lana each got a bunk to herself. You would think they'd like that; but they had to fix their own hair when Dawn wasn't home, and neither of them was any good at it. Granny Turner, on one such evening, told them to put it in twists, but the twins thought that was babyish, and Mama didn't have the patience to plait it up the way Dawn used to.

"Fix it in a bush; I'll show you how," Dude said. Dude was the peacock of junior high. He was very vain about his hair and kept a huge comb stuck in it for repairs during the day, and he checked it out every time he passed by a mirror. At home, somebody was always yelling at him to get out of the bathroom. Lena and Lana decided they didn't want that.

"I'll iron it for you," said Granny Turner, who was spending the night with them. "You're old enough to get your hair straightened."

But for once Mama said no to Granny, and the twins looked relieved. They were scared to say no to Granny themselves. They were also scared of Granny's iron comb, which smoked and smelled. Anything Granny suggested somehow sounded old-fashioned, whether it actually was or not.

"Plait it for us, Mama," Lena begged.

"Plait it your ownself," Mama retorted. "It makes me nervous."

"We can't," Lana whined, winding her arms around her like a little girl. Sometimes the twins could wheedle Mama by pretending to be helpless. Mama had a soft spot for her twins. "Please, Mama."

Granny squealed, "Don't go swinging on her, girl. You big enough to know better'n that. Where's my hickory?"

The twins exchanged a timid, foolish glance.

"And don't go cutten you eyes behine my back," Granny ordered. "I clare, Flora, don't you never learn these young'uns any manners atall? Set down there, girl, and reach me that comb."

Lena handed over the comb and crouched shrinking before her.

Granny Turner was the oldest old lady Tiff had ever known—old and mean. She lived alone in her little house in Honeycutt, and no wonder. Who would ever want to live with a mean old lady like her? You would think a lady that had thirteen children and twenty-nine grandchildren and seven great-grandchildren would be kind to anyway one of them; but all Granny cared about was money and manners. Tiff would never say so to Mama, but she liked her Granny Cox a whole lot more than she did her Granny Turner.

The plaits she fashioned were fat and lumpy and winged out on either side of Lena's head. Even Mama had to laugh. "Moo-oo," said Lena, stretching out her neck and pretending to bawl like a cow.

Dude said, "Hey, okay! Look at the devil horns!"

Granny said, "Don't you go naming the bad man in this house, boy."

"I'm going to plait me some horns like Lena's," said Dude. "Man, will I fake out the kids at school!"

Granny rumbled ominously, "I don't study the bad man in this house."

Mama said, "Quit it, Dude," but he seized the brush and deftly twisted his hair up to a point on top of his head. "Is a unicorn okay?" he inquired innocently.

The old lady bridled. "What kind of corn is that?"

Dude said, "Not corn, Granny, unicorn. A unicorn is a make-believe horse, with a horn on its head," and he pranced around Granny, shaking his head like a horse and pointing his horn at her. Tiff was scared to tease Granny. She was also a little scared when Dude teased.

Dude said, "Just one horn, Granny. That means I'm only half a devil."

"Dude!" said Mama.

Granny grabbed the brush and brandished it, and he galloped out of the room. "I don't study no devil's horns on this child's head!" she sputtered, and she brushed the horns out of Lena's hair. "Now, set there whiles I plait you up like a young lady," she ordered. "You too, girl," she told Lana. "Come a time you got to look right and behave right, and you mama don't know when that is, you old Granny learn you."

The twins sat meekly while she parted and plaited their hair in identical tufty squares, ugly, ugly. Soon after, they slipped off to their room. The old lady slept in Dawn's bed that night, so the twins dared not do anything about their hair in her presence, and they had to wear the hateful tufts in school all the next day.

"Nobody could tell us apart!" Lana raged, picking out the neat sections as she came in the door.

Lena wailed, "Everybody called us the cotton-patch twins; they thought we were being funny!"

Tiff pondered. To be called cotton-patch was insulting, she supposed, though neither she nor the twins had ever seen a cotton patch, to her knowledge. The twins liked being twins. Their twinship set them apart. They cheerfully dressed in the identical clothes Mama bought and proudly wore the cornrows Dawn plaited. But where Granny's tufts were identical, Dawn's cornrows never were, just exactly. There was always something special about each design, so that people could tell them apart without precisely understanding why. But they still couldn't tell which twin was which. A great idea came to her, something she could do for the twins, and she only needed Dawn to teach her how.

"Let's go over to Aunt Sister's," Tiff proposed, jumping up. The idea had to be a surprise, she insisted, and she made them trot most of the long way to Toadtown.

"I'm glad it's Dawn and not me that walks this far every day," Lena panted.

"Me too," said Lana. "It better be a good surprise."

An unexpected surprise awaited them at Aunt Sister's, in the form of a visitor, Joe. He and Dawn sat in the front room together, teaching a baby to take its first steps from one pair of outstretched hands to another.

"Hey, Tiff; hey, twins," Joe said nonchalantly.

"Hey," replied the twins. Tiff refused to speak. She hated Joe. Dawn didn't like him herself, any more, so why did she allow him in the same room with her, after what he did. Besides, he was ugly. He had the slick kind of black skin that didn't require much shaving, yet he allowed a frazzly mustache to grow, a few tacky hairs just at the corners of his rubber mouth and another straggle of hairs under his chin. Clean-shaven, Tiff wouldn't have given him a second glance; unshaven, he was an outrage; and every time she turned her head, there he was, fouling up her looking space.

She took Dawn into the kitchen to explain the surprise she had planned for the twins and at the same time let her know what she thought of Joe's presence.

Dawn shrugged. "Aunt Sister invited him. She says, if I like him or not, he's still the baby's father. And he's paying the bills. The doctor makes you pay some ahead, so the hospital doesn't lose out."

They went back into the front room, and Tiff sat the twins down in chairs side by side so they couldn't look at each other, and she and Dawn set to work plaiting the surprise. Joe settled himself sociably in a chair with the toddler on his lap. "Where did you learn to do that, Dawn?" he marveled, as the plaits formed under her flying fingers.

Dawn looked pleased. "Practice, mostly. Mama showed me how to plait my doll's hair when I was just a little kid, and I always liked to fool around with Tiff's, and the twins'." Tiff stole a glance at her face. Dawn was almost smiling. How long it had been! She went back to work, concentrating fiercely. "How do you get the loop to stand up and still plait it down in the same place?" She tried to follow Dawn's directions exactly.

Joe spoke. "You're a good learner, Tiff."

She did not respond. She wasn't ever going to talk to him; who did he think he was, anyway? What did he care that her sister cried and cried all the time?

He said, "Dawn's a good teacher, looks to me like."

Tiff gave him a sour glance. She'd like to teach him a thing or two.

"There," said Dawn, with a critical touch-up. "Is that what you had in mind, Tiff?"

She had to laugh and clap her hands, the twins looked so cute. Their cornrows converged in narrowing ovals to the tops of their heads, where skinny plaits stood up like little coronets in small but unmistakable script that spelled out their names:

lena lana

Aunt Sister came in to bring the mirror. "Lord, if that don't beat the hens a-rasselin," she admired. "Who thought that up—you, Dawn?"

"It was Tiff's idea," said Dawn, laughing. "What's that mean, Aunt Sister, about the hens wrestling?"

"Oh, it's just a saying Mama used to say, back on the farm."

"I love it! I love it!" Lana exclaimed. "Will you fix it this way again, when it needs it, Dawn?"

"Sure," said Dawn. "Tiff is pretty good too, and she can probably show you how, if you want to learn to fix each other's." She was still smiling.

"Mama lived on a farm?" asked Tiff. "Our mama?"

"No, I meant my own mama—Granny Turner. But your mama stay on the farm, too. We all did, growing up."

Lena said, "I don't care if they do call us cotton

patch now; it won't be because they don't know our real names."

"I didn't know Mama lived on a farm," Tiff said. "She never said."

Aunt Sister said dryly, "Might not be her favoritest place to talk about. Mama made us work, believe you me, paying off that farm."

"Where was it?"

"Why, it's still there over in Honeycutt; that's it where Mama stay right now."

"Granny doesn't live on any farm. It's just a little house where she lives in Honeycutt, with a little yard, and rent houses all around."

"But it use to be a farm. The rent houses come later where the farm use to be, I forget when. Ask Granny, next time you over there."

I definitely will *not* ask Granny, Tiff thought to herself. Get her started!

Yet ask Granny was exactly what she did, one afternoon in the middle of summer, and it did get her started and, furthermore, quickened something in Tiff that she didn't even notice at the time.

7

Bermuda Grass

Several times during summer vacation Granny asked Tiff to come help clean house, and to mow and weed the front yard for her. The house was tiny and so was the yard, and Granny wanted them both fixed exactly nice in case of company. She followed Tiff around and hollered at her if she missed a speck of Bermuda grass, and she never said please.

Instead, "Looka here, girl," she would say, "you half-jobbing there, letting that Moody grass break up my sidewalk!"

Girl was what Granny called Tiff when she didn't like the way she was doing something.

At first Tiff thought she was just acting tough. Grass was grass, wasn't it? No. Bermuda grass was different. Tough as Granny herself. It hurt your hands like wire when you pulled it, and you had to get every bit of the roots out, because if you didn't, they grew underground and came up in places really hard to get at. Like between the cracks of a sidewalk.

One afternoon in July they sat out in the yard under the persimmon tree, where Granny kept three slat chairs around a stump table, in case of company. Sure enough, Granny's neighbor, Miss Odessa, came walking down the street to visit, slowly, slowly, leaning on her cane every other step. Granny sent Tiff to the kitchen for the pitcher of blackberry tea and three glasses.

"Reach me your specs once," Miss Odessa commanded. Granny handed across her spectacles so the visitor could look Tiff over. She said, "I'd know her for Flora's girl a mile off."

"Mama says I look like Daddy," said Tiff. "We're both tall—"

Miss Odessa talked over her head to Granny. "Yes, she's Flora to the breathing breath."

"Runs her mouth like Flora too," Granny said. "All talk and no work."

No work! Tiff had just pulled about a bushel of Bermuda grass out of her old flower beds! She had no business to talk that way about Mama, when she wasn't there to defend herself. "Mama does too work," she protested. "She works every day in the factory and some more when she gets home, and it's hard work she does too. She has to fix all the broke things, sewing machine things that can't anybody but her fix. The supervisor says Mama is the best fixer they ever had."

"Huh. Best talker. All mouth, like this thing," said Granny, nodding in Tiff's direction. "Not neither of them girls worth doodly squat."

Inside her head, Tiff made ugly remarks to Granny, that she wouldn't care to say out loud. You're bowlegged, she told her. You walk like you're riding barebutt on a porcupine. You think you're smart, but you can't read or write anything except your own name. You're dumb.

What she said inside was cruel and unfair; but Granny was cruel and unfair out loud, and you weren't allowed to talk back out of respect for her age. When Tiff grew up, she promised herself, she was going to tell Granny straight that nobody liked her because she told lies about you right to your face, and for no reason except to hurt your feelings.

Yet Mama was grown up, and she didn't talk straight to Granny. She listened obediently, as though Granny still had the right. When did your turn come? You could talk back to Mama. Tiff did. They got in awful arguments, but it didn't mean she didn't respect her or love her. Tiff wondered if Mama, deep in her heart, loved Granny. Was it only the farm that Mama hated?

She spoke suddenly out of her musings, "Granny, Aunt Sister says—"

"Girl, don't butt in like that!" Granny snapped. "Can't you hear Miss Odessa talking?"

"I've finished, honey," said Miss Odessa. "What the child wanting to say?"

Granny signaled permission for Tiff to speak. "Aunt Sister told us she and Mama lived on a farm when they were chaps."

Granny nodded.

"Well, I mean, she said the farm was *here*, right where this house is. How could you have a farm in just this little space?"

"Oh, they was more of it, back then, more'n a hunderd acres; and we farmed ever bit of it."

"Mama too?"

Yes, Granny said, Mama had to plow and plant and cultivate right along with the best of them, back then. On Saturdays, she and Uncle Flake would walk into Silasville with roasting ears, to see if they could trade for a tablet or a pencil. The chaps had learned to read and write, winters, over at the Toadtown school.

Tiff regretted getting Granny started. She had heard it all before, and it was boring, boring, boring. She made an attempt to change the subject. "Where is the Toadtown school?" she asked brightly. "It's all houses in Toadtown."

Miss Odessa said, "It use to be a school in there, a one-room school. They tore it down when integration come, for the Silasville folks wouldn't want their children going to school in Toadtown."

Granny channeled the conversation back to suit her own memories. "Flake, he never liked living in the country. To this day he won't have a piece of corn bread in his house, or a drop of molasses, or one dry bean. Say he threaded enough leatherbritches he be bless if he eat one more dry bean. Where he be today, I like to know, if he han't learned to do a day's work?"

Silasville grew up around them, Granny said, and Mr. Honeycutt, the original owner, tried to buy the farm back from them. She finally gave in after Granddaddy died, but she hung on to the scrap of land the home place stood on. Mr. Honeycutt built rent houses all around her, nice little duplexes with water piped in for indoor flush toilets, and electric; but the city refused these services to Granny.

"They didn't like me owning in town, you see." She cackled spitefully. "But they had to break down and do it when it got on the Charlotte TV. The mayor, he ast them not to tell it over the TV, but they told it anyway, so I got me a commode indoors too. Flake, he hooked it up for me."

When Tiff was little, four, maybe five, she remembered going to the toilet out back of the house. Inside a tiny wooden building, she sat on a wooden bench with a hole in it, and her pee and doodoo fell through into a hole in the ground under the little building. Tiff was not allowed to go alone to the toilet, because a baited rat trap stood on the floor of the outhouse, and it could hurt her bad, Mama said. She was not allowed either, to play in the stream that ran through a deep ditch behind the outhouse, but she remembered all of them going out together one summer day to pick the blackberries that ripened on the banks of the stream, and Granny baking an enormous blackberry cobbler in her old iron stove and taking it to the family reunion at the church on Sunday. When grown-ups went to the outhouse, they were supposed to bring back a bucket of water from the branch. If you were a chap, you brought back as much stove wood as you could carry. But now the branch was covered over and the outhouse was gone, and Uncle Flake stored Granny's stove wood under the porch. The way it used to be was dreamlike in Tiff's memory, and satisfying, like stories of pioneers. Were all those good things what Mama hated about the farm?

Miss Odessa sighed. "The Lord done bless you in this house, Effie."

"I don't think He did!" Tiff burst out. "I think the city should have built you a whole new kitchen and bathroom free to make up for not giving you the electric and water in the first place. You paid your taxes same as Mr. Honeycutt! They ought to be ashamed of themselves!"

"Nst, nst, nst," Miss Odessa reproved.

Granny said, "That's the way young folks talk nowdays. Something they want, they gots to have it right now, don't matter if the Lord ready for them to get it or not. Spalled, ever last one of them, spalled rotten. Ain't Flora's chaps and Sister's and Flake's and allunem living like kings, allunem? Thowing money away!"

What she said was true, Tiff had to admit. Mama and Daddy gave them everything they asked for, long as they had the money to pay for it. They got new clothes often as anybody in school, and they went to the picture show on Saturday afternoons and ate at the Lotta Burger whenever there was the change in the house.

Mama and Daddy could have bought them a home in Toadtown, Granny accused, with all the money they had thrown away on such foolishness.

If it meant they had to live like Granny, Tiff didn't want them to buy a home. Granny's clothes came from rummage sales, and they looked it; and she saved up string and plastic bags like they were treasures. For what? If you needed a string, what she had was always too good to give away, and she would unwind length after length from the ball she had saved, looking for one crummy enough to sacrifice. You would end up with two pieces tied together, and the plastic bag she was willing to part with would be one of those tissuey vegetable wrappers with air holes punched in it. Oh, she was stingy! She never had a TV in her house until Aunt Sister gave her an old black-and-white set she wasn't using. Now she watched TV all time. She loved the giveaway shows. She had money, Mama said; she could buy herself the expensivest color set in Silasville, if she had a mind to. Uncle Flake said that was why she had money—because she never spent any of it.

Miss Odessa said, "They wouldn't thow the money away if they had to work for it, like we did."

"Mama does too work," Tiff began, "and Daddy—"

"Don't counterdict her, girl!" Granny ordered.

"I *said*, if they worked like we did," resumed Miss Odessa. "Course, we didn't get money for the work we did. Washing the clothes out by hand and hanging them out and ironing. Nowdays they all got to have they own washing machine and dryer."

Tiff said, "Mama doesn't have a washing machine."

"No, she goes to the Laundrymat." Granny spoke with contempt. "They don't get your clothes clean, those places. You look at Flora's washing, and then you look at mine, that I wash out my ownself, with some good lye soap—"

"Where you find your lye soap?" inquired Miss Odessa.

"Why, I make it," said Granny, "like I always done. I take me my grease I've saved, and lye water that it's just rain water poured through my wood ashes, and stir it up good together, and it's the finest lye soap; you can't buy good lye soap in the store no more. I tell you, it make you sick to see the grease Flora thows away, and runs right out and buys those little boxes of powder from the machine in the Laundrymat. Thowing it away! Thowing away what's bettern money just so she can spend money."

"What do you want money for, if you aren't going to spend it?" Tiff asked.

"You can look at it," said Granny. "That can give you a gooder feeling than spending it, looking at it and knowing you don't have to ask nobody for nothing. That's what I do, nights, I just take it all out and look at it."

"Take it out from where, Granny? Have you got a hiding place for your money?"

The old woman gave her a sly glance. "That's for me to know and you to find out. We worked hard for that money, me and Mr. Turner. Now there's just me for it to last my days and bury me, when my times comes. So don't ask, for I don't tell nobody where I keep my money."

Tiff shrugged, indifferent. Later that summer she was to take a real interest and an unusual part in locating Granny's money.

8

The Oral Book Report (Part I)

On a rainy Thursday afternoon at the end of July, Tiff set out with her umbrella and a peach basket full of books for the library. She felt uneasy about the oral book reports the twins warned her would be coming up in sixth grade, so although she read for her own pleasure that summer, she thought about getting stagefright and kids laughing at her every time she finished a book.

Oral book reports were scary, Lena and Lana assured her. Veterans of Mrs. Humphrey's sixth grade, they described the horrors of standing up in front of class and not being able to remember the title or the author, and of kids snickering about the way you told the plot. The important thing was not to report on the same book other kids did. Mrs. Humphrey lectured them about that, but some did it anyway. Lena and Lana always reported on the same book, but it was all right for them, because they were twins.

The library only let you take out three books on a card, but Tiff borrowed cards from Dude and her four sisters, and by doing so was able to check out a week's worth of reading on one trip. She needed her peach basket to carry that many books, but even with a basket they were awfully heavy. Fourteen hilly squares separated her house and the library, and two of the hills were very steep. Early in the summer, she devised a way of fastening a roller skate to the basket, and thereafter she found she could read on the way home, her thumb turning the pages of the book she held in one hand, while with the other she guided her improvised cart up and down the baking clay hills of Silasville. She scarcely realized the steep hills were there.

At the library that Thursday, she ran into Ms. Lackey back in the stacks, whispering with the school principal, Mr. Akers. Tiff felt shy about speaking to Ms. Lackey with Mr. Akers there, so she pretended not to see them and ducked into the next aisle of stacks. Hastily she finished her selection and carried her books to the charge-out counter. While she surveyed the drizzle outside from the steps of the square brick building, trying to figure some way of holding an open book and an open umbrella in one hand, the teacher and principal came out and greeted her. Mr. Akers whipped aloft a big black umbrella and drew Ms. Lackey by the waist into its shelter. He left his hand there on her waist while they talked. This bothered Tiff. When Ms. Lackey asked her if she was enjoying her summer vacation, she said it was okay; and when she asked her about Dawn, she said she was okay.

"I'm glad to see you keep up with your reading," said Ms. Lackey, eying the peach basket. She explained to Mr. Akers, "Tiffany was my champion reader in fifth grade last year."

"Fine, fine," said Mr. Akers too heartily, at the same time slowly stroking Ms. Lackey's waist. "That's a real tribute from one champion to another."

Now that was a compliment to them both, wasn't it? But it sounded more like a secret way of saying something to Ms. Lackey, and Tiff didn't know how to answer. So she didn't answer. Mr. Akers was a phony and everybody knew it. Faker-Akers, they called him in school.

Ms. Lackey said, "You'll be going into Mrs. Humphrey's class in just about another month."

"Yes, ma'am," said Tiff. She stared at her basket of books to keep from looking at Mr. Akers's hand on her teacher's waist.

Ms. Lackey stepped down one stair and away from his touch. "You're going to like Mrs. Humphrey a lot," she said.

"Yes, ma'am," said Tiff. She added, "My sisters had her last year. They had to give oral book reports."

Ms. Lackey smiled. "You'll find orals are no harder than written, Tiffany. And I'm sure you're already prepared. How many books have you read so far this summer?"

"Eighty-three."

"Wow!" said Mr. Akers synthetically.

"But a lot of them were those Famous Americans that are real short. One day I read five. That was the most I ever read in one day. It gave me a headache."

"It gives me a headache just to think about it," said Ms. Lackey, still smiling. "How about a ride home? You've got quite a load to manage, walking with an umbrella."

"No thank you! It isn't far," Tiff lied. "I've got to—Mama asked me to—I don't mind walking, I love to walk in the rain." She didn't intend to ride anywhere with old Faker-Akers. Hidden by the rim of her umbrella, she watched him in the parking lot, helping her teacher into his car, and his hand sort of helped her hip slide onto the front seat—it made her want to scream! She forgot about trying to look romantic, out walking in the rain, and started for home on a trot.

Denise came out of Harris-Teeter with their supper just as she was going past, and Tiff shared her umbrella the rest of the way. At home, they slipped out of their sodden sandals, and while Denise went to dry her feet in the bathroom, Tiff made herself a pickle sandwich out in the kitchen. Holding it carefully level so it wouldn't dribble, she carried it into the bedroom. There she tossed the book she had chosen to read first up into the top bunk, clenched a pencil between her teeth, and climbing cautiously, eased herself onto the mattress of her private place under the ceiling.

Safe at last! That was the way she felt whenever she climbed into her bunk. Her mattress and the ceiling were so close together she had to roll into position from the ladder, but once in place nothing could harm her. She was alone. She got out of doing dishes one evening simply because, over against the wall, she was out of sight; Dude decided she had gone somewhere on an errand or something.

She settled down to read her book till suppertime. Reading in bed that summer had become a luxurious ritual for Tiff. With a blanket folded at just the right angle for her head, she could pull a pillow across her stomach and wedge her book open between it and the ceiling, thus freeing her hands for feeding herself pickle sandwich and twisting a favorite piece of her hair round and round while she read. Whenever she finished a book, she added the title and author to her booklist on the ceiling. She had other special lists on the ceiling as well, things she wanted to be sure she wouldn't forget:

PICKLE SANDWICH

5 buttered slices of bread
1 layer of dill pickle slices
1 layer of hot pickled peppers
1 layer of pickled beets
1 layer of pickled onions

Dude and the twins said pickle sandwich looked like garbage. If too much juice soaked in, it did, sort of. Butter prevented the bread from going mushy, although a little juice sprinkled on helped to bind the whole thing together.

She had also written down—up on the ceiling—a short list of people who had given her presents on her birthday, and another one that included the name of her cousin Kenneth Turner and everybody, mostly girl friends, who had sent her Christmas cards last year. Then there was her tough list.

Her list of tough people underwent constant revision and contained some debatable entries. Mrs. Humphrey, for example, she had starred right up there with Granny and Aunt Sister, and Tiff hadn't even met Mrs. Humphrey yet. Kenneth, the New York cousin, rated a star, though Tiff still hadn't decided if he was genuinely tough or merely bragged a lot. Tiff had starred her own name back when she fixed up Dawn with Aunt Sister, but after last week's visit in Honeycutt, she erased her star and added it to Granny's.

9

It's Only Money

Lena and Dude and Lana were quarreling over their game of rummy in the front room. The TV was turned to a boisterous game show that nobody paid any attention to, while Denise, out in the kitchen, pounded meat for the chicken fried steak they were supposed to have for supper that night. Above the din, not yet absorbed in her book, Tiff's ears picked up footsteps on the front porch. Dawn coming home from Aunt Sister's? But she didn't hear the screen door open. Somebody might have knocked; who could hear a knock at the door in the middle of all that racket?

"Somebody go to the door," she yelled out. "I'm up in my bed!"

But now the rummy players were shouting insults at each other and ignored her.

"I can't go," Denise called. "I got flour on me up to my neck."

Tiff swung down from her bunk and padded through

the front room. A burly man stood outside the screen. "Your folks home?" he asked.

"Mama didn't get home from work yet," she replied uneasily. Daddy wouldn't be home that night. Thursday was his night to drive to Morehead City.

The man looked at the paper in his hand. "Supposed to pick up some bunk beds," he said. Instantly she remembered him. He was one of the men who had delivered their beautiful new bedroom furniture.

Dude and the twins crowded behind her. Tiff felt thankful to have them back her up.

"All of them? You going to take back all our beds?" Dude asked.

The man looked at the paper. "Four," he said. "Four bunks and two dressers, that's what's owed on."

Each week, a lady came around to collect on the furniture. Mama kept trying to talk her into collecting once a month, but the lady said this was the way the payments had been set up when Mama signed to buy the furniture, and if Mama wanted to change it, she would have to go down and talk to the manager. Sometimes the lady had to come back two or three times in one week to get the money. She acted pretty snotty. She said if Mama was having trouble meeting her payments, she ought to go down and talk to the manager. But even though Mama always had trouble about payments, she seemed sure the money was going to appear from somewhere. Sometimes it did. Uncle Flake paid once. Daddy paid, when he could, but most of his money had to go on the truck lease, because that was the way he made a living now, and he said if Mama couldn't keep up with all the fancy things she thought she had to have, why, she would just have to do without.

They couldn't go back to sleeping on their old double beds. The springs were still stacked up on the porch, but somebody had made off with the slats, and the mattresses got rained on one night after Tiff lined them up in the back yard so she could do her acrobatics.

"Please don't take our beds away," Tiff pleaded. Behind her, Lena began sniveling. "Mama gets paid tomorrow, I bet she's going to have the money for you tomorrow."

"It ain't me, little lady," the man said. "All I do is the hauling."

Lana started bawling out loud. The twins were too old to be such crybabies, but this time their tears didn't embarrass Tiff, for she could see they touched the hauling man. "Couldn't you wait just till Mama gets paid tomorrow?" she repeated, in pathetic tones.

"Three weeks behind already!" He shuffled a few paces along the porch and shook his head distractedly. "Now you know she's not going to catch up any three weeks of payments by tomorrow. Boss says bring the stuff back to the store while it's still good enough condition to sell used."

"Wa-ah-ahhh!" the twins wailed in duet.

"Oh, please, mister," Tiff begged, letting her voice quaver.

"What time your mama get home from work tomorrow?"

"Five o'clock," said Tiff promptly. "If you came at five o'clock tomorrow she'd be here, because her shift changes at four-thirty, and the lady that she rides with brings her home, unless they stop at the grocery store first."

"Well, you tell her I'll be here five o'clock tomorrow. You tell her, and she better pass up the grocery store and have thirty-one dollars on her, or I'm picking up those beds, five o'clock sharp."

"Yes, sir! I'll sure tell her, and I sure thank you! She'll have the money, I know she's going to have the money. She always has money on Fridays!"

The man grunted and stalked out to his waiting van without saying anything further.

"Whew!" Tiff flopped on the couch, feeling suddenly weak. "That's a nice man."

Dude said, "Yeah, but what if Mama doesn't have the money tomorrow? Lot of times she already got her pay spent up, time she gets home." He switched off the TV game show, and the room fell ominously silent. Denise came in from the kitchen wiping her hands on a cup towel.

"What's happen?" she inquired. They all began to talk at once, telling her. She did not listen for long. "Mama's not going to have any thirty-one dollars tomorrow, you know that," she said. "She already borrowed her paycheck ahead to catch up the rent last Friday."

"Maybe she can borrow ahead to catch up the furniture payments," Tiff suggested.

"No, they won't let her do that; it's not an emergency. They only let her borrow last week to keep us from getting put out of the house, because she had eviction papers slapped on her."

The twins began to snivel again.

"We'll raise the money ourselves," Tiff interjected swiftly, to keep them from tuning up. "I've got nearly two dollars left from when Granny paid me for helping her. How much you got, Lena, Lana?"

Dude had been saving over a year to buy a motorcycle, but his cycle savings amounted to only four dollars. Denise went to get her purse, and the twins contributed a dollar each of birthday money. But after it was all pooled together in a cereal bowl, after they had emptied all their pockets and purses and recovered several coins from under the couch cushions, there was only a little over thirteen dollars in the cereal bowl.

Dawn walked in the front door, accompanied by Joe. They were so engrossed in collecting furniture money they had not heard Joe's car drive up. Now that he was working the night shift, he drove Dawn home from Aunt Sister's in time for supper every night, and often he remained to share the evening meal. Mama still treated them both awful, but she never begrudged anyone a meal at her table.

They all began clamoring for Dawn to look in her purse, to search her pockets, but it was no use. She shook her head—no money. She had spent her change on Kool-Aid for Aunt Sister's kids to peddle over in Toadtown.

Without a word, Joe removed a twenty-dollar bill from his wallet and dropped it in the cereal bowl. "You want me to come over your aunt's tomorrow?" he said to Dawn.

"I don't care."

"If you wait till I get off from work, I'll pick you up in the morning and carry you over there."

"Doctor says it's good for me to walk," said Dawn flatly. She walked into the bedroom and closed the door. Joe looked after her. He shifted from one foot to the other, clearly hoping for Dawn to come out again. Presently he said good-by and departed.

Served him right, Tiff thought. She didn't intend to forgive Joe just because he had saved their bunk beds with his twenty dollars. Joe's folks didn't like Dawn; they said nasty things about her, like how the baby probably wasn't Joe's fault and Dawn ought to go to the Welfare instead of making Joe pay all the baby bills.

What puzzled Tiff was Dawn's new attitude through the summer. She did all those exercises the doctor told her to, and ate what he told her to, and swallowed a whole bunch of vitamins every day, and studied, studied, studied. Back in May when she quit school, Denise talked her into signing up for courses at the Continuing Education, and by Fourth of July she had already passed her English and math. She wouldn't have to catch up but Spanish and phys. ed. when she started back to high school after the baby was born.

Joe was attentive and spent a lot of time with Dawn over at Aunt Sister's almost every day, but she scarcely talked to him. She scarcely talked to anybody, that Tiff could tell. She spoke rudely, the little that she spoke, and answered in monosyllables, when she bothered to answer. Babies were bad for everybody, it seemed. Look what this one had done to Dawn, and how mean it made Mama, and Dawn's teachers at school, and Joe's folks. (Herself as well, Tiff had to admit. She actually disliked Joe now, and she never gave him a thought one way or the other before this baby got started. When she grew up, Tiff vowed, she was not going to have any babies, ever-ever.)

Mama came flying in the front door hollering, "Dude, Dude! I got to borrow your motorcycle money; the insurance collector's out there. Hey! Where this twenty dollar come from?"

"He's going to take away our beds, that man," Lana cried, telling the news.

Even while they were explaining about the bunk beds and Joe's last-minute contribution, Mama was gathering up and counting and figuring and rejoicing. "I can pay the insurance, and catch up my ride money to last week, and next Friday I'll use my whole paycheck to put in on the bunk beds." She swooped out the door again with the money from the cereal bowl. Denise and Dude, the twins and Tiff, all looked at each other.

"It's only money," Mama said, returning. "See, we've got all this much left over. Seventeen dollars, that be enough to get us by on the bunk beds till next payday."

"No, it won't, Mama!" Tiff despaired. "That man is serious. He says if you don't have thirty-one dollars tomorrow at five, he's going to take our beds, and he means it, I know he means it. He had his van ready to do it this afternoon, but he felt sorry because the twins bawled. By tomorrow he'll be tired of their bawling; everybody else is."

Mama bustled comfortably into the kitchen, all smiles and all compliments for Denise's supper preparations. She even spoke civilly of Joe when they sat down to table. "How come you didn't ask your young man to eat with us, Dawn?"

"He's not my young man," said Dawn.

"Not your young man! I'd like to know why, with you sitting there in the family way! Seems to me like, for how he's showing himself responsible, you acting mighty proud. Where you going to, Miss? Come back here and eat your supper."

"I'm not hungry," said Dawn.

Mama jumped up and started after her, with her face all set to holler, but something seemed to change her mind, and she sat back down in her chair at table, muttering. She glanced around at their stony expressions and smiled. "We still got seventeen dollars to pay out on the bunk beds," she said coaxingly. "He won't turn that down tomorrow. You'll see. There isn't anybody that likes to turn down money. I'd be tickled to death if somebody'd give me seventeen dollars."

"It's only money," Dude sneered.

"Well, I said that, and I meant it, too. Money don't mean anything to me."

"Yeah, we saw how you grabbed it for the insurance, and your ride, and talking about how we can pay the rest on the beds."

"That's different. I got to pay for my ride or I can't get to work, but the money, the, the, the money, that don't mean anything. I be glad to work for no money atall, if I know I can feed my family and get them the stuff they need, but money? Just money? Who cares about that?"

"Granny does," said Tiff. "Granny likes to have it around just to look at."

"If that's all she ever wants," Mama snorted. "I had me a gutful of stingy when I was a chap at home. Me, what counts is my family getting as good as anybody else in this world, and you chaps got to admit that's the truth. Granny got money to sit home and look at, sure, but when she walk out, her clothes look like she some kind of refugee."

"Well, the man isn't going to take her bed away, anyhow," Tiff argued.

"Honey, that man's not going to take your bed away. Don't you worry your little head about that. Your mama wouldn't let anybody take her chaps' bed away from them. When he come around tomorrow, I give him this seventeen dollars and he'll take it and be tickled to get it, you'll see."

Mama was right. At least she was right about the man taking the seventeen dollars. He didn't sound tickled. He sounded mad. He talked loud and stomped the porch, and Lena and Lana bawled, the big bawlbabies, and Mama promised sure to pay the whole balance on the bunk beds the following Friday; and after all the loud talking and bawling and promising were over, the man drove off with the seventeen dollars and Mama turned away from the door just as pleased with herself as she could be, and said, "Now see, what did I tell you?"

10

How Toadtown Got Its Name

The second Sunday in August was their family reunion. Everybody was coming this year, Mama's sister from Detroit and her brothers from New York and Washington, and all their families; and of course there would be Granny and Uncle Flake and Aunt Sister and the sisters and brothers from Rowan County and a lot of other kinfolks that it wasn't clear to Tiff how they were related.

All the boy cousins were billeted at Tiff's house, because Mama said it was Dude's turn to have some boys around for a change, instead of a houseful of sisters. Aunt Sister took the little babies in at her place, and the girls all went over to Uncle Flake's, except for Tiff. Mama made her go stay with Granny, to help her get ready. It wasn't fair, but Granny wouldn't let the twins come with her, or any of the girl cousins. She said she was too old to put up with a lot of smart mouths. Tiff she could deal with.

Right away she started scolding. "Another new dress! Your Easter dress would have done just as good. Flora got to go buying new and showing off at the reunion."

Tiff said, "Mama thought I needed a new dress for school when it starts."

"That's not no school dress, that's a Sunday dress."

She was partly right—it wasn't a school dress. But you couldn't call it a Sunday dress, because Mama didn't make them go to Sunday school if they didn't want to; and they hardly ever wanted to. What it was, was a new dress for the reunion. Tiff had not asked for it. She didn't like dresses much, and on a scale of one to ten, she ten to one would rather wear her pink sweat shirts and blue jeans. Worse, she worried over the way Mama had spent all of her last paycheck on new family clothes the very Friday she had promised to pay out the balance on the bunk beds.

("Well, he can't take the beds if we're not home, can he?" Mama reasoned. "And I can't pay him if I'm not home, can I? It just so happens I got to go shopping Friday evening. I don't get the chance any other time." Sure enough, it turned out like she said. They met Mama at the shopping center on Friday and bought the new clothes and ate at the Lotta Burger, and when they came home there was a folded paper stuck under the door that said *Final Notice! Balance Due* $76. He had been there and gone, the man who had been nice to Tiff, who believed her when she promised that Mama would pay. Oh, she would so much rather do without the new dress, if she could only know that her bed belonged to her, all paid for.)

"If you mama had just half the money she thows away on you chaps, yall could be living in a nice home of your own, stead of that little rent-house."

Even if she agreed with her, Tiff hated it when Granny criticized Mama.

"Sister and Flake, now, they got bigger families than yall's, and they both payen on they own homes."

Tiff inquired brightly, "You going to make one of your good cobblers for the reunion, Granny?"

"Good money as Flora draws and Robert coining it with that truck, they could have bought them the best house in Toadtown."

"Granny," said Tiff desperately, "do you know why they call it Toadtown?"

"Cause that's its name," said Granny, diverted. "Thought you claimed to be the smart one."

Tiff let that pass. "Well, where we stay is called Swenson, and there's a Swenson family in Silasville; and where you stay is in Honeycutt, and you said Granddaddy bought it from Mr. Honeycutt; but Toadtown isn't named after a toad, is it?"

"Yes it is," said Granny fretfully, "name after Free Mary Toad."

"Free Mary's name was Toad? Like a *toad*, Granny?"

"Toad, that's what I said, *toad!* What's the matter of you, girl, you deef or something?"

Oh, to be grown up! Tiff said politely, "How do you spell it?"

"Why," Granny fumbled with her dress, adjusting the collar, "you spell it *toad*, just like the regular way of spelling it."

Too late, Tiff remembered that Granny didn't know how to spell. She had never been to school. Somebody had taught her to write her name, and numbers, but otherwise she couldn't write or read at all. All she knew how to do was count. She could count money good as anybody. "Are there any Toads living in Silasville?" she asked, trying to sound sympathetic in case the Toads had all died.

"Living, I want to tell you. Own half of Silasville that's how living! There's Gum Toad, that's the banker, Mr. Honeycutt's grandbaby he was, and Thomas Toad, that's the lawyer. There's Toads into everything. Don't tell me you never heard of Toad Mills?"

"Todt!" Tiff exclaimed joyfully. "L. B. Todt Mills?"

"That's what I said," replied the old lady irritably, "L. B. Toad."

The discovery that it was Todttown, not Toadtown, never had been Toadtown, so delighted Tiff that she refrained from telling her grandmother the name was pronounced tote, not toad. It had been called Toadtown for so long. How many people realized what its real name was?

The moment of friction passed. The old woman, reminded of the past, rambled on about old grievances, past injustice, that Tiff half-listened to, half-encouraged. Mama and Aunt Sister and Uncle Flake found these evocations wearing, and Tiff did too, but tonight she was thankful to get Granny steered away from scolding.

"How come Free Mary to have the same last name as Mr. L. B. Todt, Granny?" she inquired skillfully.

"Why, that's how they done, back then. Marryen in the Bible, they used the master's name, who they belong to." It was simple, she said: Todt's Mary, free, became Mary Todt.

She showed Tiffany the names of her ancestors in the family Bible. "There, there's the one you was named for, Fanny Turner, cept you mama had to go and fancy it up. That's you great-great-great-grandma."

Fanny Turner married Salem Honeycutt,
March 10, 1866.

Fanny. Tiff was glad Mama decided to fancy that one up. "Is this you, Granny?" she asked, reading down the line of names.

"That's me. 'Effie Millsaps married Lewis Turner, October 23, 1917.' "

"Here's your name again down here in 1922, Effie Turner m. Lewis Turner; and here's Fanny and Salem Turner, and Ida and Eleah Turner and Emerline and Wiley Turner and Elizabeth and Enoch Turner—you had a lot of weddings in 1922."

"Those was the mailman wedden," Granny said. "Before, they was just Bible marryen allowed." She explained how the mailman was empowered to certify marriages for black folks. Whole families waited by the roadside for the mailman to come on his rounds and legalize their marriages with an official paper. Fanny Turner was an old woman then, and a widow, but nonetheless she waited with her son's family and her grandson's, and was married legally at last to her dead husband.

"Was she allowed? To a dead man!" Tiffany was fascinated. "What did the mailman say?"

Granny shrugged. "She paid her money, same as the rest on 'em. Wasn't anybody, cluding the mailman, that liked to talk back to Fanny Turner."

Tiffany puzzled a problem. "If Fanny Turner married Salem Honeycutt back in 1866, then shouldn't her name be Honeycutt after that? Here in 1922 it says Fanny Turner still. And Salem Turner! What happened to Salem Honeycutt?"

"Honeycutt was a slave name," said Granny. "Fanny Turner wouldn't carry it."

"But they were all slaves, you said. If he was Honeycutt's Salem, then she must have been Turner's Fanny."

"No, she never was! No, ma'am, she wasn't!" said Granny testily. "She come from the Todts, but she named her ownself, she did. After freedom, she turned her back on bondage forevermore, and she said their wedded name was to show that they turned—Turner, see—so their children would know they were free forevermore."

So it was written in the Bible record, and again when the mailman came through: Fanny Turner, turned from bondage. Her family's name was thus changed by her proclamation, but their work went on much the same as before. Salem was a blacksmith, and in the first years of freedom, they moved wherever a landowner had forge work to be done and was willing for them to shelter in a tobacco shed in part payment. Fanny would do cooking and cleaning at the big house, and work the kitchen garden and nurse the landowner's children while doing her best to nurse her own. She bore fifteen children in all, eight of whom survived to adulthood, their lives no better than hers had been—except that they were born in freedom.

11

"I Want Kenneth"

The best part about the family reunion was fixing the food. At Granny's, that had to be done the day before reunion, Saturday, because she wouldn't allow any cooking in her house on Sunday. There were a lot of rules about Sunday you had to observe around Granny. Children couldn't play boisterous games on Sunday, certainly not cards, and nobody was supposed to talk very loud, or buy anything, or work. At home, Sunday was the day Mama got caught up with the laundry, but Tiff took care not ever to let slip that Mama went to the Laundromat on the proscribed day.

They rose early that Saturday morning—no problem there. At Granny's house you went to bed at dusk, so you were plenty ready to get up at daybreak. After breakfast they made two cakes, one chocolate and one angel food, and three lemon pies. That was fun. At home Tiff never got to do any of the cooking, because she was littlest. Granny did most of it at her house too, and all of the bossing. She was vain about her baking and wanted the credit for her cakes and pies when it came eating time at the family reunion. But she was old now and tired easily, and when the cakes were iced and the pies out of the oven and cooling, and the ham biscuits still to be made, she was willing to turn some work over to Tiff.

The old lady sat at the kitchen table and opened slices of country ham that had come vacuum-sealed in individual plastic envelopes and that would not be, she said, fit for hogs to eat. Tiff had a brief vision of a hog turning up its snout at a slice of its own ham.

"How hot must I make the frying pan, Granny?"

"Till it grabs the meat, girl. Take this here'un and thow it in. I'd like to just once before I die eat some country ham that tasted like smokehouse stead of plastic." Nevertheless, when she had finished taking out all the ham slices, she wiped their envelopes carefully with her dishrag, and laid them to one side. "Good heavy bags," she said, when she stored them in the shopping bag that held her collection. "Most on 'em so blame thin you punch a hole fore you ever put your stuff in there."

To her delight, Tiff saw that Granny was right—the hot frying pan grabbed the meat with a hiss, and the fragrance of searing ham filled the kitchen. When the skillet let go, she turned the slice to brown on the other side. A lacy rim of melting fat oozed and bubbled at the edges.

"We'll make us enough biscuits for our dinner,"

Granny announced. Tiff looked longingly at the platter of cooling ham. No use wishing. She picked up the flour scoop and turned to the huddle of big lard cans where Granny stored the flour and meal and sugar.

"Give me that scoop," the old lady ordered. "Get you to messing around and spilling and I'll have ants all over this kitchen." But she drew in her breath sharply, ladling flour into the dishpan that she used for mixing biscuits, and when she finally cut a chunk of lard into the white heap, she banged the pan on the kitchen table and stood rubbing her knuckles angrily. "Here, stir that up," she said. "You going to have to do a little work around here, for I can't do it all myself."

Gladly, Tiff rubbed the lard into the flour, pouring buttermilk and squeezing it all into a glorious mess, turning it out, sifting, patting, cutting, trying to do everything just the way Granny instructed, and getting it all wrong, to hear her tell it. When Granny's arthritis acted up, it went to her tongue, Tiff thought. She wondered suddenly if there was such a thing as arthritis of the tongue, but decided that now was not the time to ask.

The biscuits smelled so good baking, she was glad she hadn't sampled the ham ahead of time. There was enough dripping in the pan for red-eye gravy and wilted lettuce too, Granny said, and she sent Tiff to pick some of the bitter leaves still growing in the garden. She taught her how to mix half of the dripping with milk, for the gravy. Into the other half she poured vinegar and, while it was still steaming, piled in the lettuce leaves.

It made a good dinner for hungry people, biscuits and red-eye gravy and wilted lettuce.

"I may learn you to cook yet," the old lady grumbled, picking scornfully at her meal. But she ate it all, and sopped up her plate with the knobby biscuit made from dough scraps, as good a compliment as Tiff could expect to get.

Tiff ate three biscuits with gravy poured over, and one more to clean her plate, and two after that with molasses, and she would have taken another, but Granny said she didn't have to make a pig of herself, and she should save some for the reunion, for mercy's sake.

After dinner they cut up the fried ham slices and apportioned the meat so there would be a bit of fat and a bit of lean for each ham biscuit. Tiff packed all the food in corrugated cartons that Uncle Flake had picked up at the grocery store; six boxes it took. Each of the pies had to have a box to itself, so as not to bruise the meringue. Uncle Flake had promised to drive them to church in the morning, and the food was all ready for him to put in the car.

But after supper that night, Uncle Flake came around with the girl cousins from New York and Detroit and said he had better deliver the boxes to the church ahead of time. "I got me seven girls to carry to church tomorrow," he said. "I got thinking, if I pack you and Tiff in there too, won't be no room for the grub, and you know that's the most important part."

The three girl cousins piled out of the car to greet Granny. She kissed each one, and to each in turn she said, "What's your name, girl? Now, which one's young'un is you?"

Two of the girls answered her, but the third, a pale and meager child of about four years, looked at the ground without responding.

"That's Tiny, George Harvey's girl," Uncle Flake answered for her. "You remember Tiny; they came down two Christmases ago."

Tiff remembered Tiny. She had a withered arm with a twisted hand, and limp ribbony fingers. When other cousins younger than she were already walking, she sat silent in her stroller. Her brother, Kenneth, looked after her. Otherwise, she was so quiet nobody paid her much attention.

Granny said, "What's the matter of her hand?"

"She was born with it like that," said Uncle Flake.

"They got any other crippled children?"

"They got Kenneth; he's about Tiff's age, maybe a little older; he's all right, but they were afraid to have any more, scared it might turn out like Tiny."

The little girl stared at the ground.

"Reckon she can use that hand atall? Don't look to me like. Fingers is all wrong someways. Let's see you try to grab hold my handkerchief, little girl."

Tiny stared at the ground. Her lips moved.

"Little girl!" Granny repeated.

"Her name is Tiny," Tiff said.

"Well, I guess I know what her name is good as anybody," the old lady retorted. "Speak up, Tiny! I can't hear what you're saying."

Tiff tried not to look, tried not to hear. Uncle Flake and the girl cousins were as bad as Granny. They gazed at Tiny curiously, as if she were an exotic trained animal, about to entertain them with some stunt.

Tiny looked at nobody. Her lips moved again, and although her voice was very faint, because of the silence they could all understand what she said. "I want Kenneth," she whispered.

12

Granny Loses Her Specs

"There's Kenneth!" Tiny screamed, when they drove into the churchyard Sunday morning. "Kenneth! Kenneth!"

"Hesh that, child, hesh, you hear me?" Granny reprimanded. "Don't you know not to go yelling on a Sunday?"

Tiny ignored, or perhaps didn't hear, the grandmother. She leaned perilously from the window of Uncle Flake's car, calling and waving. Her face was lit up and her whole small body animated with joy. When the car came to a stop, without bothering to open the door she scrambled through the window, clung there briefly with her good hand, and dropped to the ground. In her curious, sidewise gait, she scuttled to her brother, waiting a little apart from Dude and the boy cousins gathered around the church door.

"Where's that child's mother, I like to know," Granny said.

Uncle Flake explained that George Harvey's wife, the

mother of Tiny and Kenneth, had not come to the reunion this year.

Kenneth was some months older than Tiff. He was tall and slender and elegant, with hair picked out as grand as Dude's and a dazzling smile that lighted somber, brooding eyes. Two Christmases ago he had been little and pudgy, but swaggering, Mr. Big from Big City. Thought he was smart. The other New York cousins deferred to him—they thought he was smart too. Tiff remembered his snobbish accent that made her feel like a hick when he bragged about his favorite Christmas present, a walkie-talkie. ("Wucky-tucky." Scornfully, Tiff turned the foreign sound over again in her mind.) And he bragged on himself, telling about his part in a fight his mama and daddy had got into. "I call the police on my daddy and the ammalance on my mama," he had boasted.

She watched Kenneth fold Tiny's little lame hand in his, as talking to her, petting, soothing, he led her into the church. With a thrill of revulsion, Tiff imagined those ribbony fingers touching her own. . . .

One of the ushers showed Tiff and Granny to honor seats on the second row. Granny herself wore the long black usher's dress, an entitlement from past service, though she left off her badge and ribbon since she was no longer able to perform the duties.

The usher smiled warmly at Tiff and said, "Who is this lovely young soul with us this morning, Sister Effie?"

Tiff hung her head. Her soul, she knew was fraudulent. Mama had given her a whole dollar for the collection plate, and Tiff had secretly pinned it to her undervest, thinking what a good start it would make toward paying out those bunk beds. Then this morning, providentially, Granny also gave her a dollar to be used as offering. Tiff definitely decided to save Mama's dollar for the van man. God would understand. After all, she was walking around with eighty-five cents of her own money in her shoe, earmarked for the good of the family bunks. But the nickels and dimes in her shoe hurt her toes, and the dollar pinned to her vest hurt her conscience. And the usher's kindly greeting did nothing to help.

"Answer her, girl!" Granny prodded. "You want people to think you don't know your own name?"

"My name is Tiffany Cox," she managed to mumble.

"That's a mighty pretty dress you're wearing, Miss Tiffany Cox."

Granny said, "The Lord looking at her spirit, not her clothes. Ain't no dress pretty enough to hide wickedness from the Master."

"Amen, sister, amen!"

The first amen of the day, Tiff thought, as the usher left them. Granny's church, Beulah Congregation, followed the old style, with shouting and stomping and testifying that exhausted the elderly worshipers. Not many young people attended Beulah Congregation. The service lasted too long to suit Tiff's mama, who played in her factory's softball team on Sunday afternoons. The whole family liked to go and cheer for her team when they played others in the league, but at Granny's, church was where you went on Sunday, period.

The little brick building quickly filled up with the Turner family, assembled from all over. During the testifying, Tiff set herself the problem of figuring out who all the kids belonged to. All through reunion, they ran in mixed-up groups that continually altered and never straightened out until it was time to go home. Only Kenneth and Tiny sat with their daddy. In the back row, Aunt Sister held somebody's baby on her lap and laid one arm protectively across Dawn's shoulders. Joe sat modestly on the other side of Dawn, like she qualified him for the Turner reunion. Some nerve!

The singing was wonderful. Except for the preaching, song broke out spontaneously during all different parts of the long worship service. Nobody used a hymnbook to follow the music. It occurred to Tiff that many of the congregation, like Granny, might not be able to read. Pew racks held cardboard fans instead of hymn books, and the reason for this grew quickly evident. The assembly room steamed as Beulah Congregation injected itself physically as well as vocally into the singing. Fans flapped in time to the music. People clapped the solemn rhythms. Songs that began with a meditative solo generated power and fervor in the mounting harmonies.

"Thank you, Jesus!" Granny moaned.

"Thank you, Jesus!" others echoed.

"Walking on the water, praise His name!" Granny

leaped nimbly to her feet and charged the congregation with her ecstasy, eyes closed, fists clenched imploringly.

"Praise His name!" The mighty organlike sound gripped Tiff. She felt herself united with the faithful; she wanted to shout for joy, as others did. Granny lifted her long black skirt slightly and did a sudden, staccato little dance. "Glory!" she cried.

"Glory!" cried Tiff and the others.

And the song went on.

When it died away, like distant thunder, Granny settled tiredly back in the pew beside Tiff.

After a long prayer and another song, the head deacon welcomed the visitors to Beulah Congregation and cited the Turner family reunion. Granny was a lifelong member of Beulah, and the deacon assured them that he and the ushers and the preacher took as much pride in the reunion as she did. Then he announced it was time for the collection and called for generous offerings, in honor of the Turners.

Tiff unfolded Granny's dollar in readiness. The warmed bill smelled of country ham. Granny searched her purse importantly. It would not do to appear stingy today.

"Hold this," she commanded, handing Tiff her fan.

COMPLIMENTS OF SHERRILL'S FUNERAL PARLOR, the fan read. There was a lot of writing about insurance plans and burial policies that Tiff skipped to study a picture of Sherrill's Funeral Parlor presided over by a blue-eyed Jesus.

"Hold these," said Granny, rummaging in her pocketbook. Tiff took Granny's plastic rain bonnet, its accordion folds doubled and tied by its own strings. She took her white handkerchief with lace on the hem and her flowered handkerchief and her door key on a rough, knotted string. She held her spectacles and her coin purse for her, and just as Granny drew out the offering envelope from the remaining clutter in her pocketbook, the usher arrived at their row and handed over the collection plate.

With an air of deprecating largess, Granny placed her envelope among those collected from the front row. Tiff laid her dollar in and passed the plate on, turning as she did so to give back her grandmother's belongings, and thinking at the same time how Ms. Lackey said it was a fact that Jesus wasn't blue-eyed at all, but instead was a black man; and in that single instant of placing, passing, turning, giving, remembering, her eye registered the glint of Granny's spectacles in the collection plate, partially covered by her dollar and quickly hidden by other dollars, as the plate moved from hand to hand down the row.

"Wait!" said Tiff faintly. But it was too late. The usher in the center aisle took up the plate and started it on its next journey. In the pew beside her, unnoticing, Granny replaced the handful of items Tiff had returned to her, snapped shut her pocketbook, and settled back on the feather cushion provided for the honor seats. For a moment she appeared to reflect piously; in another moment she closed her eyes and nodded comfortably. Was she asleep? In a panic, Tiff decided she had to take a chance. Losing Granny's specs so carelessly was the kind of thing the old lady would never let her forget. She could almost hear her relating the wanton act to stupidity, immorality. She thought fast. Some way she had to get back those glasses without Granny knowing. As she agonized over how to do this, Granny's fingers relaxed and her fan dropped to the floor with a gentle click. By great good fortune, it slid backward under the seat. A neighboring pew mate gave it, and Tiff, an indifferent glance as she ducked under the seat to retrieve it.

She was able to scoot back under three rows of seats without drawing attention, but when she tried to creep into the aisle, the long skirt of an usher blocked her passage, and she crawled back for two more rows, weaving in and out of legs, dodging, narrowly escaping discovery when a tot pointed and said to its mother, "Looky dere!" By the time the mother looked, Tiff had spurted out of sight under another row. Shuffling feet blocked her way into the aisle; legs crossed and uncrossed kept her dodging desperately under the pews. In a final rush at the back of the church, she brushed against Aunt Sister's leg, but she managed to slip past without Aunt Sister ever realizing what had hit her.

She sneaked into the dusty vestibule just as the opposite door swung closed on the usher returning to finish the collection in the sanctuary. The contents of her full plate had been dumped on a small table stationed between the sanctuary doors. Tiff leaped to the table and sifted through the heap of bills, coins and envelopes. Granny's specs surfaced, safe, unbroken, praise the Lord! Yes, thanks be to God! Though she sometimes doubted His presence, this just had to be His helping hand. She ought to show her gratitude with a thank offering, she decided, and she bent down and removed her slipper. She hesitated. Would a nickel seem stingy to God? Probably. If so, He wouldn't be all that impressed with ten cents. But she only had eighty-five cents in her shoe, and ten cents was a good percentage of that. More than a tithe. God only asked for a tithe, she reminded Him.

"What you up to, girl! You stealing money out of the collection? Shame on you! Where your folks? They going to hear about this!"

The second usher, entering with her loaded collection plate, seized Tiff by the arm. "I can't believe one of Sister Effie's would do a thing like this!"

"I didn't! No-n-no, I never!" Tiff stuttered. She held out her hands, spectacles in one, slipper in the other. Eagerly, she explained how she sought merely to contribute to the Turner memorial collection, and she proved this by dumping the whole eighty-five cents from her slipper onto the table.

The usher gazed dubiously at Tiff's face, at the table, at her shoe. "How I know you wasn't slipping money *into* your shoe stead of *out?* How come you couldn't take your slipper off inside the church stead of coming out here this particular time, when all this money's lying on the table and both ushers inside collecting?"

By now, Tiff had regained her wits. She had already put a whole dollar in the plate, she reported truthfully. The money in her shoe represented all the coins of her savings; and it had not been her original intention to put any of it in the collection plate, but (here she improvised slightly) the preaching had been so persuasive, and she had felt so thankful, that she had wanted to give her all. At this point, Tiff reached down the front of her dress and unfastened the dollar bill pinned to her undervest. "You can see how I wouldn't want to go showing my underwear right in front of the whole church," she explained modestly. She laid the bill festooned with its safety pin on top of the heap in the usher's plate.

"Lord forgive me, sugar!" the woman exclaimed. "Evil, evil, that's what I am, suspicioning one of Sister Effie's own of sich a sich. Oh, won't she bless me out, accusing an innocent child, and on Turners' reunion day, too!"

"No she won't, not if we don't tell her," Tiff pointed out. "Me, *I* wouldn't dream of telling her about this." (And that, she thought fervently, was the absolute truth.)

The usher snatched Tiff's bill from the pile. She dumped her plateful of offering money on the table and replaced it with Tiff's safety-pinned dollar. "You come with me!" she said, and seizing her arm in a determined grip, she marched Tiff through the sanctuary door and down the aisle to the pulpit.

It all happened so fast, she couldn't figure out what the usher intended to do with her. Confess? She was agonizingly conscious of her dollar bill exposed in the collection plate, the safety pin somehow suggesting underwear. She caught one glimpse of Kenneth's brooding eyes, and peripherally observed Granny stirring awake in her second-row pew. While the woman whispered to the head deacon, she stood shrinking in the usher's clutch, her stomach in a knot, head bowed, wishing she could faint, waiting for the next dreadful thing to happen to her, since she had no more ideas for acting on her own.

The deacon grabbed her other arm, and his voice rang out to the congregation, freshly attentive to this diversion. "Now I want yall to listen to thishere, whiles you making your reunion offering. This little granddaughter of Sister Effie has put in ever cent of her savings! Yes, she did! This sweet young soul, trying to keep from showing off, she went out of this sanctuary to make her offering privately, back there in the vestibule, and wouldn't none of us know what she done ceppen our good Sister Idella here pulled her in for an example. Now whicha ones of you wants to match that pure spirit? Think about it. Thishere is a Turner memorial offering, a one-time thing!" Even as he spoke, men were reaching for their wallets.

In her pew, Granny sat upright, lips clamped together in a straight line—her way of indicating approval. When

Tiff was allowed to return to her, she fumbled inside her pocketbook and beckoned to the usher. "Hold that," she said, giving Tiff a folded bill. It smelled faintly of country ham. She wrote her name on a scrap of paper, Effie Turner, in proud curly script. She could write her name good, could Granny, and she wanted the credit. She wrapped the bill in the scrap of paper and allowed the usher to bear the small packet away.

"Here's your glasses," Tiff whispered.

Afterward, waiting for dinner to be set out on the tables in the loblolly grove, Kenneth spoke to her for the first time. In his snobby voice, he said, "What was that safety pin for, that you put in the collection plate?"

"None of your beeswax," she replied.

13

Dinner on the Ground

The men brought four long tables from the basement of the church and lined them up for a buffet out under the loblollies. The women began unpacking the boxes of food for dinner, while hungry children milled around, eying the platters and getting in the way.

Tiff felt loyal to her ham biscuits, but a panful of fried chicken gizzards almost made her salute. Never in her life had she got all the chicken gizzards she wanted to eat! Somebody set a dish of livermush beside the gizzards. Tiff liked livermush just fine, especially the way Mama fixed it, but imagine bringing livermush to dinner on the ground, where there were gizzards and ham and barbecued ribs and fried chicken and rabbit, besides all the different kinds of cakes and pies you would ever hope to see. Three wooden freezers of homemade ice cream oozed brine under the table at the end, where the desserts were.

Dinner on the ground meant wherever at church you ate your meal.

"Ant we lucky to get this good weather!" Aunt Sister

rejoiced. The year before it had rained, and the family had to eat in the basement.

"Take a plate, now do," Tiff's mama urged. The local families deferred in honor of those from out of town; but visiting adults hung back in their turn so as not to appear greedy. The children, however, made a rush for the lavish spread.

"Get away, get away from there!" Granny yelled. "Don't yall have any manners atall?" The children scattered from the threatened switch, the older ones snickering and jeering among themselves. The little ones ran for protection to their mothers, who glanced at one another and smiled ruefully. Granny was so old-fashioned she still insisted on a children's table. In Granny's day, men were served first, and after them, the women. Children were given the leavings.

Tiff's daddy saved the day. "That's right, Mother Turner, grab you a plate here," he said. "Guest of honor goes first. Mick, you and Pet and Claudine come eat with Mother; yall don't get to visit with her but once a year. Dudeboy, bring Granny out one of them good pulpit chairs. Mother of a family big as this'n deserves the best sitten there is." He bustled around, serving Granny's plate for her, soliciting her pleasure from the bounty, urging the choicest tidbits on her. And he settled her in the big armchair a calculated distance from the table, under a splendid willow oak.

How they ate! Beulah Congregation worshiped so long and so vigorously that they were all famished. Tiff gobbled down more than her share of the chicken gizzards and helped herself to generous seconds. "There's plenty left," she apologized to one of the Detroit cousins.

"Are they good?" The girl inquired tolerantly, as of something beyond justification.

"*Good?*" But what Tiff liked about gizzards might not sound appetizing by description: the gritty blue meat, the rubbery connective tissue. "Don't you like gizzards?" she asked tentatively.

"I wouldn't know," replied the girl airily. "I never tasted one in my life."

"Never tasted *chicken gizzards?*" Incredible.

Kenneth, eating with their group, observed, "I wouldn't touch one with a ten-foot pole, much less eat one."

Mr. Big. Stung, Tiff retorted, "That shows what you know," and she offered Tiny one of the luscious chunks from her plate. The little girl grasped it solemnly in her good hand, looked at it uncritically, took a bite, chewed reflectively, and bent forward to spit the chewed mass onto the ground. Alongside the rejected cud, she delicately laid the uneaten remains of the morsel.

The visiting cousins laughed raucously at her pantomime. "Ick!" they screamed, and scrambled to another picnic site. Tiff felt herself grow warm with chagrin; but she smiled and shifted along with the group and polished off the contents of her plate. "I'm going to get me some more," she announced, jumping to her feet.

With diminished appetite, however, she sauntered alongside the buffet. Bowls of vegetables had not been touched. Rowan County families contributed these from their summer gardens, and out of allegiance to Aunt Bettie Sadie and Cousin Lou, she served herself token dabs of black-eyed peas, fried okra, scalloped tomatoes, pattypan squash, bread-and-butter pickles, sweet potatoes, greens.

"Get me some more dinner," Tiny whined at her elbow.

"Get your ownself some," Tiff said nastily. "You just spit out what I gave you."

Still the little girl held out her plate. "I can't." She dangled her limp twisted fingers in proof.

Ashamed, Tiff set aside her own plate. "You want some chicken? Pork chop? How about a roasting ear?"

Freed of her plate, Tiny ignored her and wandered along the table to sample various of the dishes. She nibbled a corn bread square and laid the uneaten part back in the pan. Similarly, she tasted the spareribs, a spiced peach, and took a bite out of one of Tiff's own ham biscuits.

"Hey, you girl! I seen enough of that!" Granny shouted, descending on them without warning. She grabbed up her switch and stung the little girl's legs with it. "Cry! That's what I mean for you to do! Child as spalled as you are never got the switchen you should agot; bout time you learned!" She gripped Tiny by one arm and prepared to administer one of her notorious "dancing lessons."

Instantly Kenneth raced up and snatched the little girl from her grasp.

"Come back here, boy!" Granny hollered, as he fled

with Tiny in his arms. "You mind what I say or I want to know the reason why."

Kenneth neither minded nor explained to her the reason why. He scurried from sight around the church corner and Granny turned away muttering.

"Who's them childern belong to?" she asked crossly.

"Now Granny, that's George Harvey's kids; I told you three times already."

"Well, where's their mother at, I'd like to know!"

Patiently, the adults explained again about Kenneth's mother, shaking disparaging heads at one another.

The old woman grumbled, "Seems like I can't remember anything from one minute to the next."

The adults looked at one another and nodded.

Later, when Tiff went off by herself to the muscadine swing, she found Kenneth down on the creek bank feeding Tiny bites of chocolate cake.

They butted in on everything she liked to do, she thought with irritation, and she turned back toward the church. But the reunion had deteriorated into a bunch of old folks reminiscing; Denise and the older crowd had gone to town to see what trouble they could get into, and the real little chaps were fooling around with Aunt Sister and taking naps under cup towels. She decided to stay.

The muscadine swing was rightfully hers, after all, for it was she who discovered it one Sunday last spring, after she had gone to church with Granny. A perfect thick rope of grapevine hung from the heavy arm of a sweet gum tree. The location was perfect too—out of sight of the church. For an idyllic hour, while Granny visited with her friends in the churchyard, Tiff practiced acrobatics on the muscadine swing. You had to make a good run from this side to get across the creek, because the opposite bank was higher; but once you made it up there, the ride back was lovely and effortless, dreamy, like a hawk tilting in the sky.

Disregarding the intruders, Tiff leaped onto her swing and made several round trips, showing off just a little, for she knew it looked easy.

"Oh!" cried Tiny at once. "Let me do it! I want a turn!"

Kenneth said, "You're too little." He really meant, You can't because you're crippled. Tiny seemed to assent. She fell silent, and the two of them watched as Tiff ran and leaped and swung across, paused on the opposite bank, and floated back. It was beautiful—peaceful and beautiful. She said to Kenneth presently, "We'll take time abouts, if you want."

"I don't want to," he returned curtly.

"Swings make him dizzy," Tiny announced.

"They do not!"

"He gets carsick, too."

Kenneth flung the last of the cake into the creek. "Stupid! You're stupid, Tiny. You always talking, and you don't know what you talking about!"

Tiff let go the vine and approached him. It was evident that he regarded carsickness as sissy. The subject was of some interest to her. Lana and Lena were always claiming to be carsick so they could sit in the front seat. Whenever Uncle Flake took them riding in his car, Mama made Tiff sit in back, and the twins had to be let sit in front so they wouldn't throw up. Tiff resented this privilege. The front seat moved along same as the back seat did, she contended, and she welcomed the chance to consult an expert on the matter.

"Do you throw up if you don't get to ride in the front seat?" she asked.

"None of your business. Tiny doesn't know what she's talking about. I never got carsick in my life."

"He do! He do! He do so too! He gets carsick!" Enraged by the loss of her cake, Tiny began flogging her brother with her good hand and chanting to punish him.

Kenneth fended off her puny blows with an indolent arm. "He do, he do, he do so too," he mimicked. "You sound just like Old Lady Turner."

Tiff was shocked. "Granny doesn't talk like that!"

"*Getaway, getaway, getaway from that there table,*" Kenneth cawed.

His imitation did sound like Granny. But it was cruel of him to make fun of her.

"She can't help the way she sounds. You won't sound so good yourself when you get old."

"Maybe I won't, but I don't care how old I get, I'm not going to go round beating little kids to keep them from getting anything to eat."

"Granny wasn't trying to keep anybody from eating. Why, she worked hard all day yesterday cooking so there'd be a gracious plenty for everybody, she said so herself." Tiff began to explain about the men eating first in the old days, because they had to get back to the fields. She told how, at the women's table, Granny used to put aside the best parts of her food for Uncle Flake and Aunt Sister and Mama, so that they would have good things too when it came time for them to eat.

"Oh yeah?" Kenneth sneered. "That old woman never saved nothing for nobody."

"She did! Mama told me so!"

"Well, your mama saying don't make it so. That's an ugly old woman, ugliest old woman I ever saw. She walks like this–" and Kenneth imitated Granny's bow-legged hobble.

"You stop that!" Tiff shouted. "She can't help how she walks. You ought to be ashamed of yourself, making fun of my granny."

Kenneth did stop, and he did look ashamed. "She's *my* granny too," he reminded Tiff.

A sudden splash ended the altercation. Under their startled eyes, Tiny struggled in the shallow creek. Quietly, while they quarreled, she had undertaken to swing across, but a feeble start failed to gain her the opposite bank. Scrabbling with her feet toward the shaly bank, her grip on the vine quickly weakened and she had had to let go, dropping into the shallow pool, which her very presence dammed up and caused to wash over her.

"Get her out! She's drowning!" Kenneth screamed, grabbing Tiff's shoulder and shaking her.

"It's not deep," Tiff retorted, more amused than frightened. "Get her out your ownself."

"I can't swim! Oh, please get her out. Please help me. Oh, Tiny, Tiny!" Kenneth sobbed. His face was contorted with fear. So obsessed he was, he could not listen to her assurances that Tiny was in no danger.

Tiff seized the muscadine swing, idling in slow circles under the sweet gum tree, and flung herself surely to the higher bank across the creek. Scrambling nimbly down to the shale, and hanging onto the vine, she caught Tiny by one arm and hauled her from the pool.

"Ooh, I'm all wet," the child whimpered.

"Hold onto the vine while I get us up the bank," Tiff directed.

Obediently, the child clasped the vine. Carefully picking her way, Tiff climbed the shaly cliff, boosting Tiny ahead of her. "My, you *are* all wet," she scolded. "We better swing to the other side where it's sunny so you can dry out. Okay?"

Tiny grinned her solemn little grin. Tiff took her boneless fingers in her hand. She showed her how to brace her body against her own and reminded her to cling to the vine with her good hand. This morning she had shuddered to think of those queer, ribbony fingers touching hers. What had she feared? The limp little hand was warm, trusting. Tiff encircled her protectively, and together they floated back to the sunny side.

14

The Oral Book Report (Part II)

Mr. Big wasn't what he was like after all, not at all, Tiff learned to her amazement. Kenneth could scarcely wait to get his hands on Tiny. He grabbed her off the muscadine swing and hugged and petted her and cried (real tears, that he didn't trouble to hide) while Tiny whimpered and affected to be scared. After that, he gave her a spanking, whap, whap, but that was as faked as Tiny's whimper, not enough to make her cry. They sat on the grassy bank in the sun, and Kenneth untied her sneakers and set them on a flat rock to dry while he squeezed water out of her socks and flapped them and told her to flap her dress to make it dry too.

It was so peaceful sitting there in the meadow, with the church and the reunion out of sight over the ridge, like they were all alone on the other side of the world.

Tiny hummed tunelessly; already her soaked dress showed blotchy dry spots. She lay back on the grass and stared vacantly into the vacant sky. Presently she slept. Kenneth broke a branch off the sweet gum tree and stuck it into the ground so its leaves shaded her face.

"We're going home tomorrow," Kenneth said, looking pensive.

"Are you glad?"

"Kind of. It's nice here"—he looked around the meadow—"but it makes me feel funny when there's nobody else in sight." He began describing what it was like in New York, in their crowded apartment, always somebody around. It didn't sound so much different from Tiff's house, and she mentioned this. "Yes, but in New York, when you go out of your apartment, there's people outside too, everywhere, in the hall or on the stairs, and on the street; you can't walk someplace like this, over a hill, and get away by yourself." It was hard for Tiff to imagine. She had never been out of the county but once, on a Sunday-school trip to Virginia on the bus, and the towns they went through looked a lot like Silasville, and the countryside reminded her of Rowan County.

New York was nice, Kenneth said. People sat together on their front steps and visited, like they did here, and they leaned on pillows on their window sills and visited across the fire escapes and watched everything that happened in the street. It wasn't all just concrete sidewalks and streets, he boasted. He had an avocado seed that he sprouted in a jar of water out on his fire escape, and growing in a can of dirt a grapefruit tree that was two years old.

"Some forest," said Tiff, and he grinned.

Kenneth's grandparents lived at their apartment and took care of him and Tiny and cleaned and cooked for them while he went to school and their mama and daddy worked. It seemed strange, Kenneth having other, different grandparents. They helped with his homework and took him and Tiny to church and bought their clothes for them. His grandmother had been born and raised in the apartment building they lived in right now, and she had never been out of New York, had never seen any big bunches of trees except the ones in the parks. She knew what telephone numbers to call to complain about no heat in their apartment and how to make the city truck come pick up their garbage, and she could really bless out a cop if she thought he wasn't doing his job right. "My grandmother is tough," said Kenneth proudly.

"So is *my* granny," said Tiff.

"She's my granny too," Kenneth reminded her again.

A lone blob of cloud passed across the face of the sun, and cool sweetness invaded the heat that blanketed them. Grass heads stirred lightly, shifting patterns of green and gold and brown around them.

He began talking about the school he went to, down the street from where he lived, and he described their paved playground, enclosed by high fences and surrounded by high buildings. It sounded more like a jail than school. But in New York they didn't have to start back to school till after Labor Day.

"Lucky," said Tiff. "Ours begins the last week in August."

"Week after next," Kenneth sympathized.

"Mn-n." Week after next! It was an uneasy reminder. "My new teacher makes you give oral book reports. I never gave an oral book report before, did you?"

"Oh sure," said Kenneth, with a trace of Mr. Big in his voice. "I been giving oral book reports, I can't even remember how many times."

"I think I'll report on *Gone with the Wind*," Tiffany bragged, just to see what he'd say. She had seen the movie, after all, and she actually read a little bit of the book over Christmas, when Denise had it checked out. It was more than a thousand pages long.

"Yes, that's a good one," said he enthusiastically. "I like history things like that. Even if you know it's just a story, the history part makes it seem true."

"Like the *Little House* books." She steered the conversation to safer waters.

"Like that, yeah. How they grew all their own food and made their own house out there and stuff even when they didn't have any money."

"Mn-n," said Tiff thoughtfully. "I don't much like hearing about it, though. Granny is all time talking about how she and Granddaddy made their house, and molasses and soap, and how they never had any money, and it's boring. Even Mama doesn't like to listen."

"That's because Granny wasn't a pioneer. In *The Little House,* they were pioneers, and they were out there by themselves with nobody else to help them, and starting up the United States, and it makes you feel like you could have done it too, back then, been a part of starting everything, I mean."

"Mn-n. I guess so," said Tiff.

15

Granny Loses Her Money

The next day, Monday, Tiff was to go home. For the time of the reunion, she had postponed thinking about the bunk beds, but on Sunday night when she climbed into the lumpy bed she shared with Granny, she wondered if there would be any bed at all for her to sleep in at home, tomorrow night. She thought about the man she had deceived, coming for his money, and she stirred uncomfortably.

"Settle down there, you girl," Granny said. "Can't nobody get they rest with you threshing around in the bed."

So she lay as still as she could, not moving at all until Granny's snores liberated her; and even then she could not find a smooth place, but kept turning cautiously, lying first on one side and then the other, and thinking longingly of her bunk bed up under the ceiling, her own smooth place, hers alone. When fatigue finally released her into the privacy of sleep, she slept deeply and did not rouse when the old lady arose at dawn, according to her custom.

Sounds from the kitchen mixed in with her dreams, sounds of doors opening and closing and dreams of somebody waiting on the porch; sounds of heavy things being lifted, shifted, quickening sounds of furniture sliding, dreams of her bunk bed sliding down from the ceiling; and a queer little whickering fitted neatly into a dream she managed to shape—Tiny whimpering? herself? —whickering, whispering—what? The dream lost shape as she felt a presence, something, or somebody hovering. She woke with a small jerk to find Granny beside the bed, fumbling under the mattress. Fumbling, whispering to herself, and that queer little whickering.

"Granny?"

"My money," the grandmother quavered. "I can't find my money."

Tiff said drowsily, "Did you look in your pocketbook?"

"Not that money. My other money, that I keep."

Tiff rolled creakily out of bed and stumbled to the bathroom. When she came back, Granny had the mattress turned back on itself and the sheets and pillows jumbled in a pile on the floor.

The old lady said wildly, pathetically, "It's gone. My money's all gone. Somebody's come and took my money away from me." She began to cry, with hacking, gasping little sobs that horrified Tiff. Granny wasn't the kind of woman who ever cried about anything.

"Don't cry, Granny," she begged. "I'll help you look for your money. Maybe you just forgot where you put it. Where was the last place you saw it?"

The old lady showed her a sort of pocket in the mattress, cleverly sewed, easy to overlook, empty.

Tiff said reasonably, "Did you always keep it there? Maybe you moved it, and forgot." She opened a bureau drawer and searched through an assortment of rolled-up stockings.

"I already looked in there. It's gone, for sure, it's been stole." The old lady showed her a narrow rack, fastened to the back of the bureau drawer, cleverly fashioned out of linoleum scraps, shallow enough that the drawer could be closed, but adequate for holding a sheaf of bills, perhaps; empty.

Tiff moved everything off the shelves of Granny's closet and began searching through boxes.

"I already looked there." The grandmother now wept so uncontrollably that Tiff could not question her further. She searched the house through, moving furniture, groping inside vases, looking under rugs, checking half a dozen or more secret hiding places the grandmother showed her, false floor boards, backs of picture frames, hiding places that would have delighted her if she had not been intent on the more urgent business of soothing the distraught old lady.

"Are you sure you looked in your pocketbook?"

"Yes, but it ain't that money, it's my money that Mr. Honeycutt give for our farm, that was going to last me my days. I never kept it in my pocketbook. It's gone! Oh, help me, Lord, how'm I going to take care of me my old age?" Tears streamed down her face.

"I'll take care of you, Granny, don't worry. I'll always take care of you. Please don't cry, Granny. Let's look in your pocketbook just to make sure."

The grandmother spread the contents of her pocketbook out on the mattress. There were her handkerchiefs, the lace one for show, the flowered one for blow, her accordion rain bonnet, the door key on a knotted string, her spectacles, her coin purse. Tiff snapped open the coin purse. Inside were some coins and folded bills with a dusty look to them, smelling faintly of country ham. "Here's money, Granny."

"But my other money—my other—" Her voice broke.

Tiff studied the folded bills and figured. Something. What? "Where did this money, this in your coin purse, where did it come from?"

"Why, I take it, little bits at a time, when I need it, from my other money."

Something more, something more! "Well, your other money, you got all those hiding places you keep it in, and I figure you keep moving it around so nobody will see you going to the same place all the time."

The grandmother nodded.

"Did you ever forget where you put it the last time?"

"Yes, but I kept looking, and then when I found it. I remembered when it was I changed the place."

"Do you ever make up new hiding places to keep it

in? You could have made up a new place and forgotten, you know."

Hope struggled with irritation in Granny's face. "You think I forget where I keep my own money?"

"Well, you're always complaining you can't remember anything one minute to the next." Tiff rubbed the bills from the coin purse. Dusty. She was almost sure. "Do you keep your other money in a plastic bag, Granny?"

"In four plastic bags. How you know that?"

"Are they plastic bags that country ham comes in?"

"Yes! Yes! Those good heavy bags that they won't nothing punch a hole in. How you know that, girl? I know you never saw my money." Granny was trembling all over.

Tiff wheeled and ran to the kitchen. The grandmother hurried after her. Saturday, making biscuits, Tiff hadn't been allowed to measure flour out of the big lard can where Granny stored it. Now, she lifted the lid and plunged her bare arm inside, feeling, exploring the dusty white until she touched a packet buried there, just the way she had figured. She fished it out, and after it in quick succession, three more flat important packets, dredged with flour. "All ready for the fry pan, Granny," she teased.

Of course! the old lady said disgustedly; now she remembered. But it had given her a bad time. She sat down at the kitchen table to recover, and to fondle her money.

It was all hundred-dollar bills! Millions of them, it

looked like! First time Tiff had ever seen a hundred-dollar bill, let alone millions of them, and she said so.

Granny said gratefully, "Well, you going to look all you want, honey, for one of them hunderd dollars is yours, for a reward, finding my money for me."

"I don't want any reward," said Tiff. "All I did was help you hunt. You'd have found it by yourself, when you used up the flour."

But she might have grieved herself to death, by the time she made that many biscuits, Granny said, smiling now, holding out the reward. "Take it. I want you to have it. You get the look of a hunderd-dollar bill in your mind, and the feel of it in your hand, and you won't never want to break it down, I guarantee you."

Tiff took the bill in her hand for the honor of it, to look at and feel, but not to keep. She could understand how Granny felt, a little. A hundred-dollar bill was an important-looking thing you'd hate to break; but if you didn't break it, what was it good for? She wouldn't say so to Granny, but she'd rather be spendthrift, like Mama, buying things she couldn't afford and enjoying the spending, than hiding money away for enjoyment. "Granny!" she exclaimed, handing back the bill, "I really truly don't want any reward, but would you lend Mama seventy-six dollars instead?" She explained about the bunk beds and about the man who would almost certainly come to take them back today, and she promised to repay the loan herself, as fast as she could earn the money, or save it from what Mama and Daddy gave her to spend.

Granny snorted. "No, I'll not! Give Flora money for them beds and she'd have it spent on something else before the day's out."

Tiff couldn't argue with that. It had happened too many times before. "Well, anyway, you oughtn't to keep all that money here in your house. It's dangerous. You might get it all stolen."

"I kept it in my house all this time and hasn't nobody stole it off of me."

"That doesn't mean it couldn't happen. You thought it *did* happen this morning, and look how scared you were. You ought to put your money in a bank."

Granny began telling what was wrong about banks, how your money got mixed up with other people's and the bank people never knew which money was yours and which belonged to somebody else. Tiff didn't know a lot about banks herself, but she knew a whole lot more than Granny did. For an hour she explained the things Ms. Lackey had taught them last year, about checking accounts and deposit slips and passbooks and savings accounts. When she told how the money could earn interest in a savings account, she saw at once that the old lady was intrigued. "Any time you wanted to take your money out, a little bit or all of it, you could just write a check," she urged.

The grandmother fingered her precious hoard and

looked sullen. "That's the thing," she admitted. "I don't know how to write but just only my name."

"You can write numbers!" Tiff said. "You're good at numbers. Anybody that can write numbers and their name can write a check." She offered to go with her to the bank and do the talking, and to her satisfaction, the grandmother agreed. When had Granny ever listened to her? It made Tiff feel like she counted for something. Real tough.

"Wait," she said, as Granny put on her hat. "Count your money before you take it to the bank."

"I don't need to count it. I know how much there is of it."

"Well, count it anyway. Ms. Lackey says you ought to always count your money before you do business, so in case you make a mistake, you don't go blaming the other fellow."

Granny made her turn her back so Tiff wouldn't find out how much money was in the plastic bags. Listening to the dry shuffle of the floury bills, Tiff felt a twinge of regret that she hadn't accepted Granny's reward. There were so many of those one-hundred-dollar bills, Granny would never miss one. But she went over her reasoning once more and decided she had been right: she was content with her refusal.

"I'm ready," said Granny. She snapped the packets inside her pocketbook and stood up. "Let's go."

16

Banking

The way it happened, Tiff didn't have to do the talking for Granny after all. They arrived at the bank a few minutes before opening time, but they didn't have to wait. A roly-poly man with a fringe of gray hair and a fringe of gray mustache, unlocked the thick glass front door and let them in. "Miss Effie!" he said, hugging Granny and laughing. "I bet I haven't seen you in twenty years!"

He was Mr. Montgomery Todt, president of the bank. Gold letters spelled out his name on the door of his office, where he led them, but Granny called him Gummy, for she had nursed him as a little chap when he couldn't yet say his own name.

"This here's my grandbaby; she the smart one," Granny said, shoving Tiff forward. "Say something, girl. Show Mr. Gummy how smart you are."

Mr. Todt saved her by pronouncing roundly, "She already said her smarts, Miss Effie. A girl that could get an old pack rat like you to put her money in the bank just bound to be smart as they come."

Granny giggled at him calling her a pack rat, but Tiff didn't appreciate it one bit. That was her granny he was making fun of, even if she *was* a pack rat.

Mr. Todt asked one of the bank tellers to open a savings and checking account for Granny while she waited in his office. "Where did you get all that money, Miss Effie?" He seemed surprised when Granny told him the money had come from his own mother's father, years ago. "I didn't realize Honeycutt was your homeplace," he said thoughtfully. "No doubt Grandfather told me, and it slipped my mind. I used to listen to him by the hour, back then. Kids today never listen to old folks the way they ought to. I bet a chap as bright as Tiffany here doesn't either."

"Mr. Todt," said Tiff on a sudden hunch, "do you know where Toadtown got its name?"

"I never thought about it," he said. "I imagine it has something to do with Free Mary Creek running through there, probably a lot of toads in it." (Was it possible he didn't know the difference between toads and frogs?)

It turned out that he didn't know how Free Mary Creek got its name, either, so she told him. Bankers didn't know everything. He said his grandfather undoubtedly told him and it slipped his mind.

Granny signed her name in five different places for the bank, and she watched closely when the teller showed the amount deposited. "Wait a minute," she said, and took Tiff aside for a whispered conference. "She says I give her a hunderd dollars more than I did!"

Tiff said, "Ask her to count it again, in front of you."

The grandmother did as she was told. Carefully, slowly, the teller counted the money. "Is that correct?" she inquired.

"If you say so," said Granny. With joy she returned to Tiff. "They giving me a hunderd dollars just for putting my money in here."

"No, they aren't, Granny; you must have made some mistake counting it at home."

"I made a hunderd dollars, just for walking downtown here!" she marveled, not listening.

The old lady was so delighted that Tiff gave up trying to convince her of her mistake. At least it got her banking off to a good start.

Back at the house she set about teaching Granny to write checks. She showed her the place to write in the amount and the line for her signature. "When you get those two lines filled in, any store or person you're paying the money to will write in their own name, if you ask them to," she assured the old lady.

"Let me practice it once," said Granny. "I got a place where I want to pay some money to."

Proudly she wrote her signature, in the round, careful letters she used to sign her social security checks: Effie Turner. Laboriously, in her trembling script, she wrote out the numbers and pushed the check across the table. "You write the rest for me," she directed with a smirk.

Nobody could question the legibility of her handwriting. There stood her name, plain and positive as Granny herself: Effie Turner. Her numbers looked like first grade numbers, but they were equally plain: $76.00.

"Write it, The Outlet Furniture Store," Granny ordered.

"Oh!" was all that Tiff could think to say immediately. She thought of her bunk bed and her private place up at the ceiling, saved. She thought, humbly, that she didn't exactly understand how she felt about money—a little like Mama, a little like Granny, not much like either of them. She would have to figure some more on that one.

She could scarcely see to write the words, but she did write, blinking, as carefully as Granny wrote: Outlet Furniture Store.

"Now you hand that to you mama," said Granny, "and tell her I say she don't have to pay it back, for I already made me a hunderd dollars today."

It was the best reward Granny could have given her, since she still seemed to think Tiff deserved a reward. And it wasn't money loaned that Mama could spend on something else.

"Thank you, Granny," she said meekly.

The old lady clamped her lips tight—her way of showing she was pleased. "Guess you ain't the only one that can figure things." She closed her checkbook importantly. "Now help me find where I'll keep my bank stuff, and after we eat our dinner and clean up around here, I want you to pull that Moody grass out of my flower beds. You done just about half a job last time you was here, and I want you to make it right fore you go home."

Home! Tiff scarcely heard Granny's scolding. She couldn't wait to see their faces at home when she waved that check in front of their noses. What a homecoming it was going to be!

17

Seeing Stars

Well, what had she expected, fireworks? Trumpets, with a big ta-da! when she walked in? Of course not; but it wouldn't hurt for somebody, anybody, to say hey. Mama had already come home from work when Tiff walked in, and Aunt Sister was there on the couch beside Dawn, and Dude fiddling with the TV and Denise ironing, and not a one of them gave her a look when she carried in the brown bag that had served as her suitcase, the check for the bunk beds folded in her Thtupid sweat shirt on top.

"Hey," said Tiffany.

Mama said, "He's got a good job, Joe has, draws good pay, you got to say it."

"Big deal, factory work," Dude sneered

Denise rounded a shirt collar over the tip of her board. "Third shift," she commented.

"Fits in real good, like one of the family, I said it many of a time."

"Not in the beginning, you didn't, Mama."

Tiff said, "Hey, I'm home."

"In the beginning, in the beginning!" Mama said. "That isn't anything to do about now! Joe says he wants to get married and I say he'd make Dawn a good husband. He been steady all this time, and it's not like he cut and run soon as he find out she're expecting."

Aunt Sister spoke up. "Like I said before and I say it again, Dawn be better off if I take over the baby, when it's born. That way she can finish her education and get a job and go on and live her normal life. I been wanting me a baby, my chaps all big now. You know it'd have a good home, and no trouble, for I've always got a houseful of them to look after."

Dude said, "Who's it belong to then, you or her?"

"Me," said Aunt Sister. "That's the best way, it's the only way to do if she want to go back to living her normal life. Where I live on the other side of town is so far away she wouldn't hardly ever see it, and it would be better if she *didn't* ever see it; she could go back to the way she was before, like nothing at all ever happened."

She was right, Tiff thought, immediately absorbed in the discussion. She had been wanting Aunt Sister to take the baby all along (either her or Joe); it was the humane way, for she was the only one that really wanted it. Things were working out so well! Good old Thtupid! She stroked the sweat shirt folded on top in her paper bag and thought simultaneously of the check folded inside; and just as she thought of that, there came a thump-thump of heavy footsteps on the porch and the bump-ump-ump-ump-ump as he knocked, and there peering through the screen door at them stood the man from the Outlet Furniture Store.

"MamaMamaMama, I've got the money!" Tiff whispered. "Granny gave it for the bunk beds!"

Mama's face lighted up. "Don't say anything," she muttered in Tiff's ear. "I'll put him off with ten-twelve dollars." Mama's light went out when Tiff handed over the check instead of cash. But she paid off the furniture man handsomely, apologizing for the delay and explaining about the circumstances of their family reunion that had prevented an earlier settling of the bill. After he left, Tiff held the floor for a while as she told about Granny losing her money and getting the new bank account. Then Aunt Sister said she had to be getting along home and she'd like it decided about the baby before she went, and right quick they were back in the debate again. In the middle of it, Daddy came in, hungry and hollering for his supper.

"Feed me, feed me," he implored. "Feed me fore I drop."

They set out the stuff left over from the family reunion, best instant supper he ever laid his teeth around, Daddy said. Tiff filled her plate with yesterday's vegetables and mixed them up together with her meat the way she liked to do, the way that made Dude pretend to throw up. Tonight nobody noticed.

Daddy said to Dawn, "Honey, is that all you going to eat?"

"I'm not hungry," said Dawn.

"People going to start saying we don't feed you round here."

Dawn said, "The doctor says I'm okay."

Mama said domestically, "She'll get back her appetite cooking for Joe, when they get their own little place."

"What's all this?" said Daddy, and the argument erupted again, but hotter this time, with Aunt Sister yelling about Dawn leading a normal life and Dude and Denise cutting down Joe and his job and Mama screaming how important it was for Dawn to get married.

"Get married?" Daddy looked confused. "Who said anything about getting married?" The argument blazed forth. "Wait a minute! Wait a minute! *Wait a minute!*" The hollering subsided and he turned to Dawn. "All this talk, getting married, giving away the baby, seem like everybody putting their mouth in. What you got to say about it?"

"I don't know," Dawn said in a low voice.

"Anybody ask what you want to do?"

"No. . . ."

Mama said swiftly, "What you mean, no? Joe ask you if you want to get married, didn't he?"

"But it was more like—it wasn't what—" she chewed her lip despondently, unable to explain.

"You still don't know," Daddy suggested, and she shook her head.

Mama said, "Well, it's a decent thing Joe asked her, and I think if she was a decent kind of girl she'd want to get married. Believe you me, if I was her and in the family way, that's the first thing I'd be thinking about."

"Flora, this child isn't but fifteen years old! Just barely fifteen years old, do you call that old enough for marrying?"

"My own mother got married when she was fifteen!"

"Yeah, and Mother Turner wouldn't hardly let none of you girls out of the house till you was eighteen!"

Mama flared, "Wasn't none of us that got married because we had to, neither! Too much freedom, that's what it is. Believe you me, it wasn't like that when I was growing up."

Daddy said reasonably, "Yeah, but you thought Mother Turner was mean and bossy when you was growing up, and you still do." He said to Dawn, "You go long and don't listen to none of this stuff. The only thing in this world you got to think about right now is having that baby."

Dawn said hopelessly, "But sooner or later, after the baby comes, I have to decide."

"No, you don't. You're not but just a little girl still, and you're still *our* little girl, that we taking care of. We'll take care of that little baby, too—our first grandbaby! That's a pretty big thing, the first grandbaby. We got to start thinking about it, where we going to put it. Dudeboy, how bout you and me seeing if that lumber out back will make us a bed for the baby."

Denise said, "There's some pretty furniture scrap that Uncle Flake put under Granny's porch for kindling. You want me to run down while it's still light and bring some back?"

Aunt Sister said, "Well, I think yall making a big mistake." She looked around belligerently, still hoping, but Daddy patted her shoulder kindly. "Mistake's done gone and forgot about, Sis." He turned to Mama. "Alls we thinking about now is what's best for Dawn, right, Flora? That's always what we trying to do for our children."

Mama said "Huh!" but not very seriously, and shortly, pouring more iced tea, she said, "I gave all the baby clothes away when Tiff grew out of them. We'll have to go look at layettes after work on Friday. They got some cute things for babies at K-Mart. I know one thing sure, we're going to use Pampers this time. I said after Tiffany, I'd washed my last didey, and I meant it."

Dude said, "Boy, I sure hope it's a boy."

Later, snug in her nest up under the ceiling, Tiff brooded about the baby the family now accepted so casually. All her plotting had gone for nothing. They were going to be stuck with an ugly, squalling baby. There wasn't room in this house for a baby!

"Hey!" Tiff suddenly accused the ceiling, "Who's been messing with my booklist?" Somebody had blue-penciled her line of books. Somebody had added *Gone with the Wind**** at the bottom; it was easy for her to guess who that somebody was. Mr. Big. In a few places he had drawn a disdainful line through her book titles; but to others there had been added a condescending check mark. Probably checking the ones he had read. It did not mollify her that *Little House on the Prairie* was also starred. Her private place, up under the ceiling, had been violated. Dumb Yankee!

She vaulted out of her bunk and padded out to the kitchen. Dude was in there, spreading peanut butter.

Tiff said, aggressively, "Who slept in my bed when all the boys were here at our house?"

"Kenneth," he replied.

"I thought so. Dumb Yankee."

"Well, he a pretty smart dude," said Dude consideringly, "cept he ate a pickle sandwich last night and say he liked it. Man, it was cool here without any girls around."

"Cool mess. You just about wrecked our room."

"Yeah," said Dude nostalgically. "You shoulda heard Mama yelling, the whole living time. One fight, Hank busted Neesie's pillow—whew! Don't tell Neesie. I sewed it up good as new."

"You think Neesie's not going to notice it's all foam crumbs over the floor?" She opened the refrigerator door. "Where's the beet pickles?"

Dude shrugged.

There was half a jar of Aunt Bettie Sadie's pickled okra in the fridge. Tiffany used those on her sandwich instead. Not bad.

Climbing back up in her bunk, she found more of Mr. Big's handiwork. He had starred his own name on her tough list. Conceited! He wasn't so tough; look how he cried, when Tiny fell off the muscadine swing and he thought she was drowning. On the other hand, Granny cried when she believed her money had been stolen, and if Granny wasn't tough, who was?

Before she could think that one through, she saw stars, two blue stars by her name on the tough list, and Pickle Sandwich****. That dumb Yankee. Maybe he wasn't as dumb as he looked.

18

The Oral Book Report (Part III)

School began the last week in August. Dude started in at high school with Denise, and the twins moved up to junior high. Back in elementary, Mrs. Humphrey assigned oral book reports to sixth grade on the first day of school, exactly as the twins had warned she would do; but she said they could report on any book they had read during the summer, and she allowed two weeks preparation before they started giving their reports. Every day of the two-week period Tiff changed her mind about the book she was going to report on.

"Just be sure you don't sign up for the same book somebody else does," Lena reminded her. "She grades you off for that."

"What if you only read one book and somebody else read it too?"

"That's your tough greens. It wouldn't matter on a book report you hand in, because everybody hands in the same time, but with orals it's easy to copy somebody that reports before you do. That's why she grades off."

She couldn't grade that hard, Tiff thought, or she wouldn't have promoted Lena and Lana.

On the last day for choosing, she put down as her selection *The Little House on the Prairie*, and that very same day, D.B. Holsclaw, the clown of the class, signed up for *The Little House on the Prairie*. So Tiff erased her title and wrote in *The Little House in the Big Woods*. Right away D.B. said he had changed his mind, and he wanted to report on *The Little House in the Big Woods*, and he wrote it in carefully as a second choice.

"You're doing that on purpose," Tiff accused him angrily.

"Doing what on purpose?" D.B. inquired, wide-eyed.

"Who's doing what on purpose?" said Mrs. Humphrey, the disciplinarian, joining them at the bulletin board where the book titles were posted. Mrs. Humphrey was a large, strict lady who put on her glasses when you answered her questions, like she was listening to you with her eyes. The habit unnerved Tiff, but D.B. responded with aplomb.

"We're just trying to keep from signing up for the same book, Mrs. Humphrey."

The teacher nodded. "You're both good readers. I've seen your summer reading lists. No reason for either of you to duplicate."

As she walked away, Tiff with a spiteful glance at D.B. wrote *Gone with the Wind* on the list as her second choice. Let him top that one.

Mrs. Humphrey called on D.B. first for his oral book report. He stood up in front of the class grinning, with his hands in his pockets, and reported on *The Little House on the Prairie*. He gave the name of the author, and he told who the characters were and he said it was about the old-timey days when not much happened, no Indian fights or anything like that. He rocked gently all the while he spoke, grinning, hands in his pockets.

He's scared, Tiff realized. In spite of herself, she sympathized.

Mrs. Humphrey asked, "Did you enjoy the book, D.B.?"

"Well, it was kind of boring back then, I guess," said D.B. "but it was okay." He swaggered back to his desk.

Mrs. Humphrey asked if anyone would volunteer to give the next report, and to Tiff's surprise, she found herself raising her hand.

She stood in front of the class, heart pounding. She felt faint. This wasn't like any written report, not anything like it at all. "*The Little House on the Prairie*," she heard herself saying in someone else's voice, "by Laura Ingalls Wilder."

Mrs. Humphrey looked puzzled. "You're reporting on D.B.'s book, Tiffany?"

"Yes, ma'am." She added rapidly before the teacher could say anything, "D.B. told who the characters are in this book, so I won't tell about them. I just want to tell about the part I like that isn't boring, really it isn't, where Laura says about how they made their own house and things, back then when there wasn't anybody to help them."

She described to the class how the land looked on the prairie, the unfolding miles of grass where nobody had lived before them, and she told about the meager Christmas that had drawn the pioneer family close together. "They were really poor," she explained, "but it didn't matter because in their family everybody worked together to help out."

"That's very interesting, Tiffany," said Mrs. Humphrey. "Do you think people are like that today?"

Tiff thought about her own family, how they had all yelled and argued about Dawn's baby, but in the end they were all working together to help Dawn. "Yes," she said. "They don't have to build their own house any more, like the pioneers did, but they still stick together, and sometimes they make things they don't have to, just because they always did it that way. My grandmother makes her own soap. It would be easier for her to buy soap, but that's what she did when they didn't have any money to buy soap, so she's still making it for herself. She says her soap is better."

Tiff told how Granny poured water through wood ashes and mixed it with grease drippings and stirred and stirred until it became soap. She grew aware of the quiet and the class listening intently to her words. Even D.B.

was listening. Oral book reports were easy! All you had to do was talk about something important.

She told them how Granny's house used to be out in the country, until Silasville grew so big that the farm became part of the town. She told how Granny's sons and daughters had to walk to Toadtown, to school, and how Toadtown got its name, and Free Mary Creek. She told how her ancestors chose their own name, Turner, because they had turned their back on slavery. "They never moved out of this county," she concluded, "but they were pioneers too."

Mrs. Humphrey said, "That's an excellent report, Tiffany, an excellent collateral discussion." She gave her an A on her report—her first for the school year. When they were going out for recess, she complimented her again on her collateral material. "You may write a book yourself, some day," she said.

"Well," said Tiff, "I've been practicing for an acrobat, but maybe I could be a book writer too." She wondered privately if you could be a writer if you didn't know what "collateral" meant. She would have to look it up, for she didn't feel like asking quite yet; and even if she did, Mrs. Humphrey would probably just tell her to look it up. She was a good teacher, but she wasn't anything like Ms. Lackey.

Ms. Lackey had been transferred to high school this year. She was teaching remedial reading there. Denise said they had moved her out of elementary because she was too friendly with the principal, who was a married man. Tiffany was indignant. "How come they didn't transfer Mr. Akers, then? He was friendlier to Ms. Lackey than she was to him."

"But Ms. Lackey is a woman," said Denise.

"You mean, no matter which one is friendliest, they would still blame Ms. Lackey just because she's a woman?"

"That's right. Just because she's a woman."

"That's not fair," Tiff protested.

"You can say that again."

Since school began this year, Denise talked a lot about women standing up for their rights. Some other girls in high school talked that way too. They were getting up a club, and Ms. Lackey had already promised to be their sponsor. In free period, girls congregated around Ms. Lackey, Denise said, just the way they used to in elementary.

It was a good year for Denise, this senior year. Early in September she was elected homecoming queen; and she was also running for student council. Tiffany felt proud when people asked her about her popular sister. The Cadillac agency was going to give her a car to drive around in during homecoming week, and she would ride in the parade, and between halves at the football game, she would walk out on the field with her arms full of flowers, and they would sing the school song and put a crown on her head. The whole family was going to be there to watch.

But two days after she was elected, Denise stood up

in assembly at high school and resigned from being queen. She thanked everybody for voting for her, but she said she had thought it over, and she wanted to do more in school than just be a symbol. She said what she really wanted to do was to work on student council to represent everybody in high school fairly, and she hoped everybody would vote for her for that instead.

Tiff was shocked when Denise came home and told what she had done. "You've got to be crazy!" she said.

The twins were disgusted and disappointed, and Dude was downright mad—his first year in high school, he said, and the way Denise acted made him feel ridiculous. While they were reproaching her, a reporter from the Silasville newspaper came to the house and asked if she could take Denise's picture. A queen resigning was news, she said. She talked to Denise a long time, and they all hung around and listened. It wasn't that she told the reporter anything different from what she said in assembly, but somehow, hearing her say it again changed the way they felt. The reporter interviewed them afterward, and they all said they were proud of Denise; and that was the way she wrote it up in the newspaper.

The next day, the TV station in Charlotte sent two people to their house to interview Denise, a woman to do the interviewing, and a man with a portable TV camera to make the movies. First they talked to Denise and made a lot of pictures of her, and then the woman asked if she could interview the rest of them. Lena and

Lana got stage fright in front of the camera and backed out, but Dude clowned around and said he was thinking of running for homecoming king himself. Tiff said, "I think my sister is like a pioneer. If there weren't ever any pioneers, people would be still living like they were back in the Dark Ages."

The most fun was looking at themselves on the six o'clock news that night. Denise looked great. They showed her explaining why student council was important to her and homecoming queen wasn't, and they showed her sitting at the kitchen table pretending to study, and they showed her coming out their front door with a jacket thrown over her shoulders, pretending to start off for school. Then Dude came on the screen, grinning and picking out his hair while he talked.

"Look at Dude!" Daddy said.

"There's Tiffany! Listen!"

"I think my sister is like a pioneer," the TV Tiffany said in somebody else's voice, but plain and easy, not at all self-conscious. It was like an oral book report. It was like she went on television every day as a regular thing.

19

Marchers in the Parade

"Oh. Oh. *Oh.*"

Tiffany paused at the front door and listened. It was one of those sparkling Carolina days, when the crisp October air seems to clear summer out of the house forever; not winter yet, not for weeks, but the good, sharp promise of it. The chill of the house together with the unexpected cry that greeted her made her shiver.

"Oh-h-h!" came the cry again. It was Dawn.

Tiff ran into their bedroom. Her sister lay in the bottom bunk. "Dawn," she exclaimed, "was that you crying?"

Dawn smiled sheepishly. "I didn't go to scare you. I thought everybody was at the parade."

"They are. I ran home to get Neesie's cash box that she forgot, while they looped around the court house. Her club is selling taffy apples—why is your face so wet?"

On the floor beside the bunk beds a newspaper had been spread out, with a ball of white string on it, and Mama's sewing scissors, and the heavy brown bowl

Mama used for mixing corn bread, now filled with water in which a wash rag floated. Tiff looked at the wash rag, trying to figure out why Dawn didn't go to the bathroom to wash her face. Then, comprehending, "Is it the–?"

Dawn nodded. "Baby coming. Pretty soon, I think." Something blurred in her eyes, and her expression concentrated, like someone straining to pick up a far-off sound. "Uh," she whispered, "uh-uh-uh-uh."

"Pretty soon? Oh, Dawn! You've got to go to the hospital! I'll run next door and call the ambulance, I'll get somebody. . . ."

Dawn was not listening. Her eyes squeezed shut, her teeth gritted, she turned her head from side to side on the pillow. Tiff stared, mesmerized, frightened. Did Dawn actually mean to have the baby by herself, without help? Tiff knew she had to do something, but she was afraid to leave her sister now.

"Listen, Dawn?" she tested. "Listen, I want to go for help, do you hear me?"

The restless turning eased, ceased. Dawn sighed and opened her eyes. She smiled ashamedly. "I'm sorry. It's not like that all the time. And it's nothing but a bad stomach cramp, or a backache, I can't tell which. After it's over I feel okay again. It's not too bad, anyway." Sweat shone over her face.

"I'm going next door, I'll only be a minute."

"They've all gone to the parade. Nobody's home."

"There must be somebody home," said Tiff, thinking

fast: the telephone in the Laundromat, three blocks up the hill.

"There's not. I already looked. It's okay, Tiff, I don't mind. Pioneer women, you know, they didn't have any hospitals." Dawn again smiled with an attempt at bravado that wrung Tiff's heart. Her darling sister, who petted her, and plaited her hair, and rubbed her back when she felt lonesome. That odd blur was beginning in her eyes again. Tiff, scared as she was, knelt by the bunk to reassure her. "Hold my hand, Dawnie," she soothed. "Squeeze it hard as you want to, you won't hurt me. Don't worry. Squeeze hard, harder, you're not hurting me. Squeeze that old pain away." On and on she murmured in her sister's ear, trying to sound confident, wishing for someone to tell her the right thing to do. Presently Dawn relaxed her grip and sighed.

Tiff was beginning to understand the rhythm of her pain. What she didn't understand was how they were supposed to use a bowl of water and the string and scissors; and she suspected that Dawn didn't know much more than she did. Pioneer or not, she vowed, Dawn was going to the hospital. Tiff would figure some way of getting her there. "Do you think you can walk?" she asked.

"Oh, sure, I been walking around the house all afternoon. I'd have walked to the hospital if I'd known it was going to take this long. But I was scared the baby would maybe fall out in the street. All of Aunt Sister's babies were born at home," she added, as Tiff led her toward the door. "I can't make it to the Laundromat phone, if that's what you're thinking." She clung to her arm. "Don't go away, Tiff. Please? Promise you won't leave me alone."

They stood in the doorway looking out, Dawn breathing in shallow gasps. Tiffany felt cold. Swenson Street lay silent, deserted, like the picture of a ghost town. Blocks away she could hear music, and faint drums that paced marchers in the parade. Mama had reached the court house by now. She had promised to meet Tiff and the twins there right after work.

"I won't leave you," she told her sister. "Don't be afraid." All the while her eyes were searching, searching —for what she did not know.

"Uh," Dawn grunted, "uh-uh." It was beginning again.

"Let go my hand a minute," said Tiff. Far down the hill, her eyes found what they were searching for. The blue light of a police car coming up Swenson Street. "Hold this!" she said, grabbing Dude's pillow from the couch. "Hold it tight. Tighter! Stick your face in the pillow and yell! It'll make you feel better. Yell loud!"

Dawn buried her face. Tiff flew out of the house, waving her arms at the racing police car. It gave no sign of slowing, and just as it reached her house, she lunged from the curb, as if to cross in front of it. Tires wailed, the car skidded and jerked to a stop, and a man bellowed out at her, "You crazy kid, you! You could be killed doing a fool thing like that!"

Tiffany said swiftly, "Officer, my sister is about to have a baby. Help me get her to the hospital."

The man's anger evaporated when he saw Dawn clutching the pillow in the doorway. "I'll radio the hospital for an ambulance," he said.

"Please, can't you drive her there yourself?"

"Girl, the ambulance won't take long to get here, and they're all equipped, and besides, I can't do it, I'm on orders from the station to go to the parade."

Tiff took a breath. "Listen," she said, "my sister isn't but fifteen years old, and there isn't anybody around but her and me, and no phone or any way to get help. If you leave us here, I'm going to tell it, that you just left us to go to an old parade. To the newspaper and the TV and everywhere, I'm going to tell it. I'll write down your car number, and I'll tell."

"*Tiffany!*" Dawn screamed.

Instantly the police officer sprang from the car and raced to the porch. "It's all right, Miss," he told her. "Lean on me. We'll get you to the hospital. Everything's going to be all right."

Between them, they helped Dawn into the police car. She was sobbing and nervously clenching her fists. "I don't know what's happening," she apologized tearfully.

"Don't you worry," said Tiff, taking one of her hands in her own. "Everything's going to be all right."

The car flew along familiar streets, but their urgent pace and the siren blaring and the officer reporting the emergency detour to his dispatcher made the trip seem unreal. Listening to the officer calling in gave Tiff an idea. "Can you call other police cars on that phone?" The officer nodded, and she proposed, "Could you call up to the court house and tell them our mother is there and ask her to come to the hospital?"

"Girl, there's a couple thousand people at the court house and only one car on duty there. How you expect one police officer to find your mother in that crowd?"

"The mayor's supposed to make a speech," Tiff persisted. "I bet if they asked him to and told him Dawn was having a baby, he'd make an announcement over the loudspeaker. Tell him Mama's name is Flora Cox." In her mind she added, And don't call me girl; but she didn't say that aloud, because the man was already talking into his microphone again and she could hear him saying "Flora Cox. You got that name? Flora Cox. Say that her daughter is having a baby, and for her to come to the hospital right away."

Tiff fought one last battle in the admissions office, where they refused to let her accompany Dawn to her room on the ground that she was under sixteen years of age.

"Why does she have to go up there alone?" Tiff argued. "Dawn isn't but fifteen years old, and she's scared to go by herself. All I want to do is stay with her till our mama gets here. . . . Besides, I am sixteen, so I can go with her."

"No, you can't, because I know you're not any sixteen years old."

Tiffany took a deep breath. "You don't know that, or anything else about me. My sister needs somebody to go with her." She was about to threaten them with the newspaper and TV, when the door opened and Mama walked in.

"Oh, Mama!"

"Oh, honey! Dawn, Tiffany, my sweet girls!" And they all hugged and cried a little, because each had been badly frightened in her own way, and nobody had wanted to say so.

20

"You Name It!"

Tiffany trudged home from the hospital. She flopped on the front porch, and then jumped up when she saw some kids in band uniforms ambling down the hill, swinging their instruments and chattering. Lena and Lana would be home soon. She hurried inside to dump the water from the brown mixing bowl and put away Mama's scissors and string. She didn't feel like explaining.

They arrived in a bunch, Neesie, Dude, and the twins, all talking at the same time, telling how the mayor called out Mama's name on the loudspeaker and questioning Tiff. She could not force herself to share their excitement, and she responded so dully, drained by the events of the afternoon, that they finally left her alone.

But it was a special time, and they wanted to do something special. Denise went in and made up Dawn's bed neatly with the best flowered sheets. Dude carried in the wooden bassinet he and Daddy had made and set it in front of the TV. Lena and Lana talked about fixing supper. Almost as if he had planned it that way, Daddy drove in early from Morehead City, and they rushed to tell him about Dawn. He didn't hang around to hear the whole story, but drove off to the hospital in the truck without even washing up.

The life of the household sparkled and swirled. The twins announced that they were going to make a pie, and Denise went up to the Laundromat to telephone Aunt Sister.

Tiffany climbed into her top bunk. For a long time she lay on her side, staring at the wall. She wondered idly if she would have been capable of helping Dawn get the baby born, if that police car had not come along. She decided yes, she could have done it if she had to; that was the way things worked. You were always running up against new situations that nobody told you how to handle, and something always happened, you could always figure a way.

But figuring a way usually made you feel good, and Tiffany didn't feel good now, not one bit. It was the baby, she recognized that. There was something nasty about this baby, something wrong. It was Mama staying mad at Dawn for so long, and Dawn changing, and Joe butting into their family—crummy Joe that nobody liked very much. That baby was Joe's baby, it had no business butting into their family. They were getting along just fine without it. Joe would have to take it away, she decided grimly. There would be some way of making him take it; you could always figure a way.

Footsteps sounded on the front porch, familiar footsteps. Incredibly, Mama and Daddy came in the house, laughing and talking and telling the news. Reluctantly, Tiff climbed down from her bunk and drifted into the front room.

Dawn had given birth to her baby, Mama announced, almost an hour ago.

"Yow!" said Dude, "What's she going to name him?"

"Her," Daddy answered, smiling. "It's a baby girl."

"Tiffany!" said Mama.

"Ma'am?"

"That's the baby's name—Tiffany," said Mama. "Dawn named her after you."

Tiff was outraged. "She can't have my name!" she blurted. She amended, "I mean, we'd get all mixed up, if it had the same name as me."

"Well, you name it," Daddy said. "Dawn wants you to. She says you maybe saved the baby's life, so she named it after you. You're supposed to pick out a middle name to call it by, so you don't get mixed up."

"Look, it's still light outside," Dude marveled. "We went to school today, and the parade, and Dawn had a baby, and it isn't even dark outside yet."

"And we're making a pie for supper!" the twins remembered, rushing for the kitchen.

It *was* queer, that so many things could happen in one day before suppertime. Tiff went back to her bunk and began making a list of middle names. She would pick an ugly one, for the ugly baby. Joe, she thought spitefully, that was an ugly name. Joe; Josephine?

Mama and Neesie carried the new bassinet into the bedroom. Mama put a pillow in for a mattress and Denise fixed it up with a plastic pad and one of the new blankets from K-Mart. They rearranged Dawn's bureau drawers to make space for the baby's clothes, and Dude ran to the grocery store for a box of Pampers.

"How long will Dawn stay in the hospital?" Tiff asked.

"Oh, about a week, I guess," said her mother.

"A week! She can't get well in a week, can she?"

"She wasn't sick, you know," Denise said. "She was pregnant."

Mama said, "They don't keep women in bed the way they used to. They found out it was better for them to move around. Dawn had an easy delivery, and the baby is strong, the doctor said. I spect he'll discharge them next Saturday, or Sunday, maybe."

Sunday, Tiff said to herself, make it Sunday. The later the better.

But before noon on Saturday, Joe drove Dawn home in his car. He parked carefully out in front and jumped out and ran around to hold open the door for Dawn. He took from her the blanketed bundle she was holding on her lap and held it awkwardly as she got out of the car. They came into the house together, Dawn walking slowly and looking very different from her old self. She was thin now, of course, and that made a difference. Tiffany ran to greet her. "You're thin, Dawn!" she exclaimed, almost afraid to touch her. "I don't mean just thin in the stomach, you're really skinny!"

"What you think we trying to get her to eat all this time for?"

"Are you all right, Dawn? You look so different skinny."

"We'll fatten her up," Daddy promised.

Dawn smiled abstractedly. "Put her in the bassinet, Joe. Look, she didn't even wake up."

They gathered around, suddenly solemn, to inspect the new baby. Tiny! Could a creature that tiny be a real person? Just a week old, and already a real, separate person! She had about a bushel of black hair curling around her little round face, and she didn't actually look babyish at all. She lay slumbering, her womanish little arms extended commandingly, her exquisite fists seeming to clutch a royal scepter, perhaps, her perfect lips working slightly, as if making a silent pronouncement to her loyal subjects.

"She looks like Dawn," they said; and politely, "She looks like Joe, too, around the mouth." "Tiffany," they tried her name, "Little Tiffany."

Dawn said, "I'm going to call her by her middle name, so they don't get mixed up. Tiff's sposed to name her. Did you pick a name yet, Tiff?"

Everybody looked at her. Josephine? she debated. Tiffany Jo? It wasn't really an ugly name; cute, actually.

And Joe, gazing solemnly into the bassinet, somehow didn't look so ugly either.

The baby opened her eyes gently and delighted them with her soft, unfocused gaze. She was *theirs!* It was amazing, this composed little being was one of their family! Tiffany uncurled the plump fist tentatively. Delicious little fingers gripped hers. "Wa-a-a," declared the infant angrily. They laughed and praised the remarkable new baby, who already knew her own mind.

"Call her Turner," said Tiffany, inspired. "I want to name her after great-great-great-great (she hesitated, unsure of her greats) grandmother." She expected somebody to challenge the number of greats, but nobody did. Instead,

"*Turner?* You can't call her Turner. That's a last name. It isn't a girl's name."

But it had been the name a girl chose, so long ago, a spunky reminder, for her, and for the new person. (She could tell her, Tiff thought, she could talk to her when she was old enough and tell her about her proud name.)

Dawn said, "*I* think it sounds like a girl's name. I like it."

And so she entered their lives, because she was theirs, and became one of their family, and was called Turner.

21

Moody Grass and Simmon Pudding

The first frost killed the Bermuda grass; Tiffany wouldn't have to pull that again for a while. The first ripe persimmons fell. Granny gathered them up, but there weren't enough for a pudding, so Tiff said she would climb the tree out front and pick some more. It was a lovely tree with branches so nicely spaced she could swing from limb to limb like she was on a trapeze.

"Now quit your stunting and pick them simmons, if you're agoing to!" Granny called. From high in the tree she looked merely small and anxious down there on the ground. She wasn't so tough.

Tiff said, "Watch this, Granny," and she ran a couple of bouncy steps along a great spreading branch.

Granny screamed "Oh!" A shower of fruit fell around her.

"That's enough, that's enough," said the old lady

nervously. "I said *pick* them, not thow them at me. Get down from there and help out a little, once. I'm not going to do all the work myself."

Tiff dropped out of the tree. Squish, a persimmon skidded under her sneaker.

"Now look what you done!" Granny scolded. "Don't you never do anything right? Bad enough to go clambing around in trees, girl as old as you are." She made Tiff pick up and cap the fruit, and then she made her carry the garbage can around to clean up the yard. "I don't study sliding around on mashed simmon all winter," she said, and she took the fruit inside to sieve for the pudding.

But Granny's arthritis hurt her fingers, and she made pitiful faces while she pressed.

"Poor Granny, I'll do that," said Tiff, taking over. The nicest-looking persimmons, the firm ones, were still puckery and made Tiff's mouth screw up. They really needed another frost to sweeten them, but Granny said they'd taste all right in pudding. Sieving them was hard work, there were so many seeds, and the pulp was sticky, and you had to mash and mash to get it to squeeze through the sieve holes. Still Tiff wouldn't let Granny do it, even when she declared her arthritis had stopped hurting. Tiff knew her Granny.

"Go on, quit now, girl," said the old lady. "You got right much squoze out, we'll get a fair taste for supper."

Tiffany worked on. "Might as well make as big pudding as we can," she said, "in case of company."

Granny said, "Well, hurry up with your smearing around and get out of my way, then whiles I mix it, for I'm not letting you go messing my kitchen."

Tiff just grinned and measured out the flour and sugar and mixed the pudding herself and poured it up and set it in the oven to bake. She did mess the kitchen pretty bad, and Granny yelled about it, but so much of Granny's yelling was obviously fake; you couldn't worry about it.

Granny's old friend and neighbor, Miss Odessa, stopped by to visit a minute or two right at suppertime, and Granny made her stay and eat with them.

"My," said Miss Odessa, "if that don't beat some of the best simmon pudding I ever put in my mouth."

"Well, this girl here made it, ever bit," Granny said. "I was plumb give out myself, and I told her, Quit now, girl, I told her, but shoot, this thing is Flora to the breathing breath, going to do just the exact opposite what I tell her to. Stubborn! Don't ask me whicha one of them girls is the hard-headedest."

"Granny," said Tiff, "I wish you'd quit calling me girl."

The grandmother started hollering about how Tiff wasn't too smart for switching yet, but Tiff scarcely listened. She was coming to see that a lot of Granny's scolding amounted to a kind of family compliment.

"You know, Granny," she said, trying out a compliment of her own, "you talk awful puckery, but you taste okay in the pudding."

BELINDA HURMENCE has worked in an Army hospital, in a petroleum testing laboratory, for a Wall Street insurance corporation and a paper company, and on two New York magazines.

But it was while she served as a children's librarian that she became aware of the scarcity of literature about black children that could offer them a sense of recognition. "*Tough Tiffany,*" she says, "is my drop for that bucket." This is her first novel.